Sorcery Cold

Sorcery Cold

A Fairytale for Adults
Part 1
Bari in Inari

by Helmut Barthel

translated from German by
Riocard Ó Tiarnaigh

German National Library Cataloging-in-Publication data: The Deutsche Nationalbibliothek lists this publication in the Deutsche Nationalbibliografie; detailed bibliographical data is available via the internet at http://dnb.d-nb.de

Helmut Barthel, Sorcery Cold, Part 1
© Helmut Barthel
All rights reserved

Rights for this Issue:
MA-Verlag, Stelle-Wittenwurth
ma-verlag@gmx.de
1. English Edition 2017

Typeset, layout and envelope design:
MA Publishing House
Picture credits:
All black-and-white drawings
by the author, © Helmut Barthel
Maps: Beate Schwab,© MA-Verlag

ISBN 978-3-925718-38-0

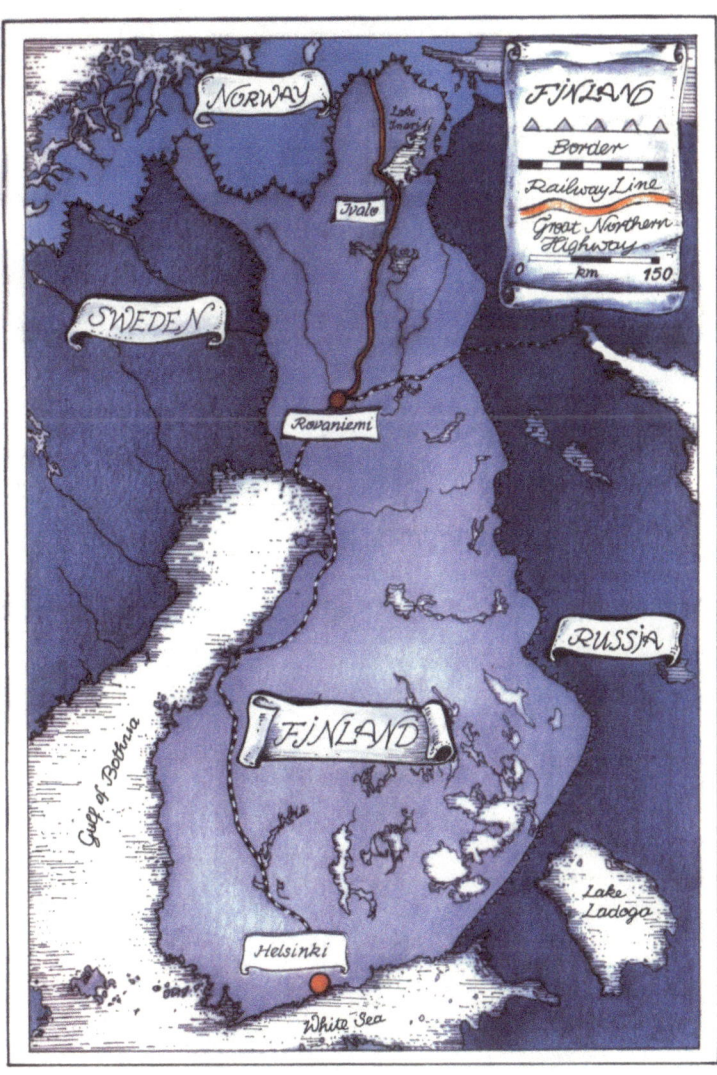

Follow me now on a trip into the past, which nonetheless is as close to the future as the words I am going to use, in order to relate the events of my trip to the sources of magic. (H. B.)

Contents

Prologue

The Beginning of the End
or A Fairytale for Adults

It is eminently possible, that my memories have lost their sharpness or that I confuse somewhat the circumstances, times and places of important and even random events and encounters. I'm not even all that certain, whether I haven't frequently experienced things quite differently to others, who were with me in the same situation. Undoubtedly, however, the thread of my personal fate has become inextricably entwined with that lineage, whose credibility and exactitude render the objections vis-à-vis its implications and its validity null and void. Being the mother of all unfinished battles this lineage nourishes itself from reality.

On the basis of this conclusion, everything I have to report can be taken as an authentic and fair account of actual events. In this spirit, I would like to tell my story, starting at the beginning for as long as my pen guides me and my memories keep me awake.

The Plastercast
(Part 1)

I'd landed myself in trouble. The last bit of paraffin, which I'd brought with me in my lamp to be on the safe side, I'd already used up. I'd burnt it foolishly in a last attempt to set alight the wet branches and sticks. The wood, which I'd stacked up for a fire, was so wet, that not even the faggots would ignite. The last match was wasted in a fruitless attempt to turn the soaking woodpile into a raging campfire. My hands and clothes reeked of paraffin and the continuous, wet and cold rain only seemed to magnify the stench.

At this time of the year the evenings could barely be made out and night had almost engulfed the horizon. After a last glance at my manual disaster in all its dreadful consequences, I set about doing quickly what was necessary to weather the oncoming darkness without a fire.

Although the temperature was probably a couple of degrees celsius above zero, the cold dampness, the result of relentless, penetrating drizzle and the marshy ground near the lake, where I'd made my camp, was all-encompassing and left no room for regret or reflection. I would have to make the best of a bad lot.

In concentrating upon the problem of trying to light a fire, I must confess, that I had completely forgotten to set up my little tent before dark. As a result, I had no option, but to make do with my sleepingbag in a hollow between the roots of a large pine tree, which I was just about able to make out by the dim light of my torch. With my rucksack placed between the tree's trunk and roots, thereby forming an improvised rain cover, I squashed myself into the recess of this primitive hole in the ground and, oblivious to all fear, fell fast asleep in no time.

When I next opened my eyes, I found myself sitting in the very rowing boat, with which I had earlier conveyed myself and my camping gear across the lake to one of the little islands. Earlier the boat had been lying on the shore opposite the spot with the pine tree hollow, into which I'd crawled during the gloomy night. Although it was overcast, foggy and pitch black, I could just about discern subtle differences, shadows or movements in the air and follow them with my eyes. Without my torch, which I had probably left behind in the hollow under the large pine tree, I was unable to visually get my bearings. Instinct, more than anything else, kept me sitting there in the rowing boat. It wasn't the noise of human feet or animal hooves on the ground, which held my attention, nor was it the outlines I merely suspected, nor sounds of breathing, which seemed to indicate a sentient being in my proximity, but rather the distinct feeling, that someone or something was contesting the space around me and hindering my movement, which commanded me to absolute silence.

The light rain had given way to a fog. It seemed to me as if the air and everything else - apart that is from the wet trees, bushes and broken pieces of wood in my vicinity, the rippling lake under my feet and the wet seat under by backside - had gotten somewhat drier. Nevertheless, I was surprised to see sparks of light coming from the direction of the camp fire, to hear increasingly the crackling sound of branches and twigs catching fire and to glimpse a warm and flickering blaze, which in the surrounding darkness could almost be compared to the sudden rising of the moon with its silver glow.

At the edge of the brightly burning fire stood a figure in a thick cloak. It was small of stature, not more than one and half metres in height, yet was too stocky and certain in its movements to be a child. This discovery, along with finding myself suddenly inhaling the thick smoke of burning wet wood, rendered me incapable of keeping up with the rapid ongoings at the edge of the fire. With its shadowlike appearance the person managed both to deny comprehension as well evade my searching glance. Its magnificent head of hair, comparable to an oversized Afro, burned itself onto my retina.

I took a deep breath of smoke and had to cough terribly. In doing so, I wakened with a start and found myself gasping, growling and spluttering back in the hollow of the pine tree trunk. In the course of my coughing fit I had pushed my rucksack off to one side. In front of my eyes a roaring fire blazed, where earlier, I don't know exactly how long before, had lain the heap of wood, which had caused me such grief. Although the fire radiated heat and light in abundance, it was a while before I managed to clamber out of the hollow and sit in front it.

The Plastercast
(Part 2)

I adjusted my parka jacket, set the hood back in place and fixed my gaze on the miraculous flickering. There were numerous reasons for me not to look around and check out the situation more thoroughly. First and foremost, I had to come to my senses.

The dream experience prior to my awakening seemed an understandable consequence of the body having to somehow get some sleep and recuperation under the inhospitable circumstances pertaining. It appeared more than plausible, that the inhalation of pungent smoke had caused me to dream about a fire and someone lighting it. The origin of the fire, which at that very moment was consuming my pile of wood, remained concealed in the flickering flames. No flight of fantasy, however bizarre, could induce me to speculate, as to how the remains of unseen embers had managed to set the wet pile of sticks on the slippery ground alight. Under the circumstances, I wasn't interested in thinking as decisively or purposefully about this riddle, as it deserved. Of primary importance for me was warmth and my decision, to remain awake until daybreak by whatever means necessary.

I must have fallen into a very deep sleep. Even as I slowly began to realise, that the telephone ringing was pulling me back to reality from other spheres, it took me quite a while, before I rolled out of my low-standing bed, sat up and vigorously rubbed my eyes. On the other end of the line was Herr Kruse, the owner of my favourite antiquarian bookshop, one which specialised mainly in literature and second- and third-hand books. Our longstanding relationship as vendor and customer had made me one of the chosen few, who Herr Kruse, if he thought it might be of interest, kindly supplied with book order or delivery information, in advance of the merchandise reaching the shelves.

On this occasion Herr Kruse was calling for a different reason. He enquired about a small relief, which he had given me at the end of large book purchase as a little present, so to speak, and in the belief, that it would give me particular pleasure. The outline of the relief showed a smith at work. At the time Herr Kruse gave it to me, it seemed fitting, as some of the books I had bought dealt with the subject of ironwork, artisanship and the like.

"I just had a customer in the shop", he said to me, who, in a book about Norwegian handicraft, had been surprised to come across an illustration, which, if his memory was correct, had to be the exact image of the relief, which he previously had bequethed to me as a gift. Regrettably Herr Kruse had gotten carried away and told said customer about the relief. The latter had become very excited by this piece of information. He was downright beside himself at the prospect of actually being able to examine the relief. Herr Kruse had allowed himself to be persuaded into inquiring of myself, should I still be in the possession of the relief, as to whether I might afford his customer the opportunity of seeing it. "No problem in the slightest", I replied. I told Herr Kruse, that he could have the piece back on loan, thereby affording the customer the chance to take a look at it.

Herr Kruse thereupon informed me, that the customer had already rejected such a proposal on the grounds, that he was passing through and would only be in Hamburg for twenty-four hours at the most. As an alternative suggestion, he had asked for my address, so that he might contact me directly by mail at a later time on this matter. With things getting increasingly complicated, I, to my own surprise, spontaneously proposed a simplification. As I had nothing planned that afternoon, it might make more sense, if the customer were to meet up with me, thereby fulfilling his desire to see the relief with his own eyes and touch it with his own hands. All we had to do was arrange a suitable meeting place.

Twenty minutes later I found myself waiting for Herr Å. Kittelsen two doors down from my own apartment building in front of a cornershop bakery, which stood diagonally across from the Sankt Johannis church in the Ludolfstrasse in Eppendorf, which is a popular wedding venue. The bookseller would be able to give the tourist clear directions; of that I was sure.

He showed up on time on the corner in front of the baker's shop, wearing a sports jumper, outmeal-coloured corduroy trousers and weighed down by an extra large rucksack. He was taller than me, slighter in build and in contrast to my long thick hair he had none. Exactly as Herr Kruse had informed me, Herr Kittelsen was easy to recognise by his bald head, his sporty appearance and his oversized rucksack.

I addressed him and we exchanged greetings. With a short handshake and a light bow he introduced himself: "Hallo, my name is Åse Kittelsen. Herr Barthel, I presume." I nodded, whereupon he put down his rucksack and enquired immediately about the relief. I took it out of my briefcase and placed it in his hands. "It's a plastercast and not a relief; just a copy", he declared at once.

I asked him, if it contained the same motif as the illustration, which he had come across in a book in Herr Kruse's shop in the Arnoldstrasse. He nodded, repeating, "Plaster, a plastercast cast." To my question, if he was disappointed, he nodded in the affirmative. To dispel the ensuing awkwardness, I made a comment along the lines, that I couldn't imagine what might be particularly interesting about the portrayal of an iron smith working at something similar to an anvil with a striking tool. Thereupon Herr Kittelsen repeated in a very serious voice, "It's a plastercast alright, but not of an iron smith at work." According to him, it showed a person on the point of striking an earthen mound or a boulder with a heavy cudgel or club. It was the portrayal of a liberating blow, he said.

My bewilderment and the look of astonishment on my face seemed to amuse him for a moment, while simultaneously assuaging his own disappointment. In a friendlier and more outgoing tone he declared: "If you haven't understood that and would like to find out more, you're welcome to contact me via the Folklore Institute at the University of Oslo." I wanted to ask him, what the importance of the plastercast was in this context, but for Herr Kittelsen the conversation was already over.

The way he shook his head and threw his rucksack over his shoulder along with the finality, with which he thanked me for my assistance, would probably have caused most people to just leave it at that. I pursued him, however, and asked for his address, in case I should learn more about this plastercast and questions arise, with which he could maybe help me. Although noticeably under time constraints, he pulled a business card out of his wallet and handed it to me. He remarked, that he worked occasionally as an assistant in the bookshop in Helsinki named on the card. After a short expression of thanks and regret for his sudden departure, due to his not having much time until his flight, he left me standing there.

I went into the deserted baker's shop to get a bread roll and coffee. I'd only just reached the counter, when the saleswoman asked me, "Did you have an argument with that tourist?" I shook my head, whereupon she quickly followed up her question with the observation, that the guy hadn't exactly made a cheerful impression on her. "He was in a rush to catch a flight", I explained and she nodded affably.

In the hallway I bumped into Dörte from my flat-sharing community. She gave me a hand-written note, according to which Michael, a sports colleague of mine, had been unsuccessfully trying to reach me and requested, that I return his call. When I got him on the phone, he reminded me of an appointment we had, which he assumed I had forgotten. I retorted, that I was just a few minutes late; there was no need to make a big deal about it, as I'd only been out for a short period to the baker's.

He understood that, Michael replied, but while out and about he had seen me standing near the door of the baker's, totally engrossed in a lively conversation. As I hadn't noticed him, he had decided not to bother me.

"A lively conversation?", I repeated in surprise. "Yes, with that big guy in the duffel coat, who seemed to be explaining something to you." I suppressed the urge to ask, what exactly had occurred, when and with whom, and instead just rearranged our appointment.

Nothing could have prevented me then from returning directly to the baker's and asking the manageress to try and recall, what exactly the tourist had looked like, with whom, according to her impression, I had argued in front of her shop ten minutes before. She looked at me coldly and stated unequivocally, that I had been there ten minutes earlier and had bought a bread roll and a coffee from her, before disappearing in a hurry. She hadn't noticed any tourist or a dispute with one.

A telephone call to the antiquarian bookshop brought no clarity into the immediate chaos of spoken and unspoken misunderstandings. "A strange fellow and a little bit melancholy, that Herr Kittelsen", was Herr Kruse's only comment to my enquiries. I kept the rest of my questions to myself and simply thanked him.

At this stage, I hadn't the slightest desire to discover even more discrepancies, which then would need clearing up. All I was interested in was my coffee and my bread roll. I left the piece of plaster, on which everything had turned, almost deliberately unattended. I would later come to regret this, as despite the greatest of efforts, I was never able to find it again. By the same token I must confess, that I only started searching for it many weeks later.

The occasion was a fireside chat amongst friends, in which each of the participants recalled a strange event or a peculiar incident. The plastercast would have been the perfect artifact for a dramatic rendition of my little story. Unfortunately the plastercast was no longer in my possession, not even as an aid for a funny story.

At various moments, sometimes unexpectedly and for no particular reason, my thoughts would return to the lost piece of plaster and the image imprinted in it. More than anything it was the claim by Herr Kittelsen, that the relief didn't depict an iron smith at work, but rather a person with a heavy cudgel or club carrying out a liberating blow on an earthen mound, which preoccupied me.

To the same extent in which this liberating blow sparked my imagination, it also remained a puzzle. For that reason I would have loved to have been able to examine the plastercast again under a magnifying glass.

Half a year later, a girlfriend and I had come the conclusion, that it would be of great artistic, professional and cultural value to spend a long period, to be more exact the entire winter, in the far North. Our preference was the Arctic Circle, with all its challenges and beauty. Unfortunately the pre-Christmas hustle and bustle prevented us from immediately realising the plan.

For myself and this girlfriend the thought of researching a book on the subject of shamanist cultur, in particular of Sami shamans, and the attraction of taking a break from the usual constraints and social activities, while working creatively for a while in completely different surrounding contributed to the decision, to pursue such a project regardless of the obstacles.

As additional justification I persuaded myself, that if we travelled via Finland, I could always visit the bookshop Herr Kittelsen had mentioned. Although in the meantime I'd managed to lose the business card he had given me, the address in Helsinki had remained in my head.

The decision was quickly finalised. Despite all the hectic activity involved in preparing ourselves for the coming adventure, in the little time remaining we had fun explaining our intentions as best we could in our social circles.

Anyone, who has ever set off on such a trip, knows the excitement and the tension, particularly that of leaving heavy burdens behind.

Faster than expected or than we could have even prepared for we found ourselves in Helsinki. Although tired and weary, we headed straight for the bookshop at the address given. It was easy to find not least, because it was located near the harbour, where our ferry had just docked. It being the largest shop of its kind in the city, the residents of Helsinki we spoke to were able to point us in the right direction. As things turned out, we didn't need the business card with the all-important address.

By comparison with the bookshops in Hamburg this one was absolutely huge. On this particular afternoon it seemed that any- and everbody, who wanted to have a read or purchase a present, was there. Having furtively and unsuccessfully searched both storeys of the shop twice, we took our courage in our hands, approached the employees and enquired after Herr Kittelsen. The name and my description of his appearance sufficed for us to be informed by two different salespersons, that such a man had never worked there, neither full- nor part-time. We stepped out into the wet and cold weather and the darkness of the streets. It was tiredness more than anything, which led us to decide, to remain no longer in Helsinki, but to continue instead our train journey northwards. The bright lights, the inviting shops, the hustle and bustle of the many shoppers, the traffic noise and the police sirens, which reminded one of Hollywood movies, were getting on our nerves. Even to stay here overnight would have been too much for us.

The modern train with its extremely comfortable compartments chugged its way ever further inland in a northerly direction. The reserved, melancholy sounding chatter of our fellow passengers had a calming influence on our mood, as did the dark night and the natural landscape rolling past the windows. An overnight stay in Rovaniemi, the capital of Lapland in the Arctic Circle, had reenergised us by the next morning. After quickly finding our bearings, in what appeared to us a satellite settlement, we knew in which direction we had to head next. In a travel agent's we rented a log cabin for an indefinite period deep in the woods at Lake Inari, approximately 30 kilometres from the settlement of Inari, and bought tickets for the next bus on the highway leading north.

The eight hour bus trip, interrupted by three half hour breaks, was taxing, but not tiring. The landscape, through which the highway led, while corresponding to our expectations, was nonetheless impressive. The further north we travelled, the more the tall coniferous trees diminished in size. Eventually the bus stopped at what looked to be a small farmstead and the driver informed his last passengers, namely ourselves, that we had reached our destination. Talvitupa, Winter House, was the name of the place. Having alighted, we found ourselves standing bemused with our rucksacks and bags, while watching the tail lights of the bus disappear into the distance.

An empty house was the only structure to be seen far and wide and in the twilight rain there was nobody around, of whom we could ask directions. We were surrounded by short stumpy trees, but nowhere was there a sign or even a recognisable path leading into the forest.

The main northern highway, along which our bus had travelled, resembled more a gravel road than the main transport artery to the most northerly towns and villages in Finland's Arctic Circle. The route, which led to our rented log cabin five kilometres further on into the forest, and which was shown on the map as a large path, turned out in reality to be nothing more than a beaten track starting and ending at the lay-by on the main highway. As we stumbled through the trees, we felt ourselves following more a forest trail than a regular path.

When we finally reached the log cabin, we found a fire in the stove and two friendly Finns waiting to greet us. They introduced themselves as members of the landlord's family and with a few words they showed us the immediate surroundings of the house and gave us instructions on how to use its various fixtures and tools.

In reply to my question, where we might get food at this time on a Friday afternoon, one of the Finns brought us around to the rear of the cabin, on the wall of which a fishing line with a hook on the end was hanging from a strangely formed branch, and pointed in the direction of the lake only a couple of steps away. The friendliness and helpfulness of the landlord's family, which in the course of our stay we would come to value, caused the two men to return after about an hour in their boat with a supply of fresh fish for us.

The following day pangs of contrition and/or self-doubt resulted in my initially not being able to start or finish anything. The sense of having perhaps erred out of spontaneity, grew with each hour. Cantankerous and sulky, I was casting about for some kind of outlet, which might relieve my sense of being at odds and ends.

Not wanting to strain our comradeship unnecessarily, the only solution it appeared to me was to withdraw for the period of reflection, in order to clear my head. To this end, I informed my partner, that I was going to spend a couple of hours alone this coming night on the island facing our cabin.

Having come to this decision around midday, my preparations were hasty and left something to be desired. I managed to reach the island in the rowing boat with an hour to go until nightfall. Since Helsinki the fine rain and the cold had become increasingly the deciding factors of my mood and it was this, which was driving me on an inward journey. In no time I was overcome by a deep sleep.

When I later awoke, the realisation, that I had forgotten something essential and important, hit me like a blow. My bones were hurting, as if I had spent the night mountain hiking. Simultaneously my heart was racing, something I was unable to get under control by spontaneous deep breathing. In the meantime the fire had gone out. A glance at the neon gray sky told me, that I had overslept the dawn.

Lapland
(Part 1)

Over breakfast in front of the rapidly warming stove, Kirsten and I resolved without further delay our argument, which had been born of frustration and tiredness. We wanted to use the morning hours concentrating on our original intention: to explore Finland's bogs, lakes and forests in the deep winter of the Arctic Circle. I was animated by a dark premonition, that of all places it was here under the dominion of the Arctic night, the aurora borealis and the most starry sky on the planet, that my hunt for long lost human lore as well as traces of abilities and expertise uncultivated by civilisation would begin.

Kirsten, despite her own inclinations, had allowed herself to become ever more infected by my single-minded drive and its gradual fruition. In principle there now was no difference of opinion between us. In the solitude of our accomodation and the peace and quiet of the surrounding lakes and forests we were determined, that nothing should distract us from our efforts to discover the essence underlying the visible world.

Nevertheless we needed the next couple of days to familiarise ourselves with the living and working conditions on-site. We were fortunate in being able to avail of the last couple of ice- and snow-free days before the big chill began in earnest. We had just managed to complete the last necessary tasks, before an overnight fall of the finest snow covered the whole forest and the little cove on the Inari Lake, at which our cabin stood. In the morning, as we looked out the large bay window towards the lake, the shore of which was roughly fourty paces away from the cabin, the white splendour filled us with delight. Immediately after breakfast I pulled the rowing boat, which I hadn't used since that night on the island, up and away from the shore. We spent this first day of real coldness filling each and every crack and gap in the wooden walls of the cabin with bits of left-over paper, in order to prevent draughts. To the same end, we hung curtains and blankets in front of the doors and windows. The temperature was down to minus twelve degrees celcius already. By the time we had arrived in Lapland, there were only five or six hours of daylight of a kind comparable to dusk at our home latitude. The increasing darkness meant, that we had to plan our routines carefully and divide up our activities into those, which required daylight, and those, which could also be managed at night.

Along with the necessary work in and around the house, one of the primary tasks, which despite the declining light had to be performed daily, was the sawing and chopping of life-giving wood for our stove. Thereafter, it had to be carried from the chopping area and stacked neatly against the wall of the cabin, in the shelter of the veranda roof, for future use.

Without much ado, we fell into the habit of preparing and eating our meals in the morning, as darkness was just lifting, and in the afternoon, as it was falling again. I was astonished, just how quickly the steadily decreasing daylight came to dictate our sense of time and led to our becoming ever more preoccupied with the completion of our essential tasks.

After dark we had as our sole sources of light the stove and two candles. Reading, writing and handiwork became extraordinarily intense activities, requiring the fullest concentration, as the candlelight made greater demands on our eyes and our other senses than we were used to in our normal lifestyle. As a result, our ability to perform these and other tasks grew exponentially as time progressed.

Once a week - we agreed that it be Mondays - we set off to the nearest settlement, which in this case was Inari, about thirty kilometres from our winter quarters, in order to stock up on foodstuffs, to hand in letters at the local post office and pick up any, that might have arrived for us. It was for this reason, that we quickly fell into the habit of writing and preparing on Sunday evenings whatever letters we wanted to post. Our day out, as we used to call it, while in itself a big deal, represented a considerable distraction in terms of time and possibilities from pursuing those matters, which for us were far more important than shopping. By the same token however, these necessary weekly expeditions afforded us the opportunity of meeting people other than the members of the landlord's family, who would pay the occasional visit to the cabin.

Naturally, I couldn't wait to start bothering the locals with those questions, which seemed important to me. By the third week of our stay in Lapland, I felt I had gotten to know a couple of people reasonably well. I was hoping, that in the course of a casual conversation, the likes of which arose while shopping in the local supermarket, an opportunity might present itself. Without a doubt, the supermarket in Inari, with its out-of-date ambience somewhere between a grocer's and a haberdashery and its little sales counter for pricy meat and foodstuffs, was a centre of communications, even if it appeared to us like a lumberjacks boutique.

On completion of our shopping and the visit to the post office, we used to wait in the local bari for the bus. Returning southwards at midday via the Northern

Highway, it would collect us at Inari and drop us off at the side of the forest in Talvitupa. It was in this very same bari, that I attempted to engage a person, with whom I had become acquainted, in discussion and put my questions to him.

By use of manual gestures and various other non-verbal skills as well as with the assistance of an interpreter I managed to communicate to the man at the adjoining table, who, whenever we had met, had greeted us in a friendly manner, that I was hoping to do research for a book and was wondering, where in the surrounding area I might come across a shaman.

The man's friendliness disappeared and he reacted indignantly. Via the intermediary he expressed irritation, that I should pose such a question. He pointed out, that we were living in the twentieth century and the conditions, in which an enquiry about such people might have been relevant, lay at least 200 years in the past. He reminded me, that the people of the locality were all good god-fearing Christians, and stated, that were it not for the fact, that I was an unsuspecting tourist, he would have held my broaching such an issue against me. He suggested, that if I was interested in good relations with the locals, I should desist from making such enquiries in the future, thereby indicating, that he wasn't merely speaking for himself.

In that moment I had a feeling of having committed a dreadful faux-pas, as the reaction I had just evoked was similar to what I might have expected, had I enquired with the utmost casualness in a German village about the whereabouts of the local witch. My facial expression of dismay prompted the man to try and make amends for his brusque remarks. In a conciliatory tone of voice, he made me aware of a regional feature, which might be of interest to me. He was referring to the existence of a state-subsidised heritage club, whose members maintained the musical and dance traditions of the locality in general and the Sami in particular. Unfortunately the regular performances of this group only took place during the summer months as a tourist attraction.

I can't say what depressed me more: the initial, almost aggressive, repudiation of my attempt to raise the subject of shamanism or the saccharine-sweet, conciliatory, yet abysmal misunderstanding with which my little lapse was to be swept under the carpet. As was only to be expected, I expressed deepest apologies for my clumsy indiscretion. While still somewhat taken aback, I thanked the man for his helpful suggestion.

Kirsten and I spent the entire bus journey back to Talvitupa as well as the five kilometre long walk through the forest to our log cabin arguing the positive and negative points which had arisen in the course of the strange and intense conversation with the man at the next table in the bari in Inari.

Much later that same night we came to the conclusion, that the strong reaction I had provoked on the part of the locals could not be put down to an aversion towards ourselves or tourists in general or dismissed as mere rustic ignorance, and that there had to be an alternative explanation for the man's sensitivity to the mention of shamanism, which to us remained unfathomable. The year was 1975, and in an era of mass media the upsurge of interest in native cultures with all its unavoidable side effects could not have left the heart of Lapland, of all places, untouched. To me it seemed self-explanatory, that a renaissance of the old cultural values, including those of sha-manism, should manifest themselves here in this region with its dependence on the tourism industry. As we slowly fell asleep, Kirsten and I, on the basis of our own in-stincts, filed the day's dispute away as being not completely resolved. Only later would I discover, to what astonishing de-gree we had come to the correct conclu-sion, while simultaneously missing it by miles.

Lapland
(Part 2)

Back in the cabin we fell into a daily routine, with which we endeavoured to make the best use of the tiny amount of available daylight. At its highest point the sun would rise just above the horizon and even then was frequently obscured by clouds. The outside temperature was bitterly cold. Our relentless time management, itself a reaction to the hostile environment and the lack of creative possibilities, initially made the regular and vital tasks exhausting. That said, we still had enough time, actually more than would have been available to us under normal circumstances in Hamburg, to concentrate our minds upon the central questions of our self-chosen mission. On occasion the pattern of the daily work routine merged seamlessly with our exertions in coming to terms with the elemental forces and circumstances of our temporary living environment.

Under such conditions extensive trips or excursions were out of the question. The dim light and the early onset of darkness didn't permit leaving the vicinity of our log cabin with its small woodshed thirty metres further into the forest and the site nearby, where a selection of pine tree trunks lay stacked, ready for chopping into firewood. In going beyond this small area for any great length of time one incurred the risk of being suddenly caught out by nightfall and of completely losing one's bearings. Even during the few hours of dim daylight, it was sometimes only possible to find one's way safely back to the cabin and its fire by means of extreme care and recourse to boy scout tricks. This we learnt the hard way on the few unavoidable occasions, in which we had attempted to go further away from the cabin and penetrate deeper into the forest.

It was for this reason, that we would use the five kilometre walk to the bus stop at the northern highway as an opportunity to explore the immediate surroundings. The rising and falling track led through a forest landscape filled with pine and other coniferous trees. Extending over large ridges of hills and smaller rocky slopes, it wouldn't have recommended itself as a cycle path or an exercise track.

While walking over snow-covered cracks as well as pits in the ground one could end up unexpectedly in an icy hollow. As a consequence, our initial excursions through the forest forced us to learn a form of movement, which previous to that would have been unknown to us. Getting from a to b required a degree of care and attention without which we wouldn't have been able to cover such dis-tances unscathed. It is therefore not surprising, that the efforts involved in our initial weekly marches, five kilome-tres to the northern highway and five kilometres back before nightfall, would leave us drained for the rest of the day.

On these initial long walks we had hoped, that we would be able to perceive the mag-ical emanations and identify the mystical features of the incomparable landscape. Certainly, there was no lack of phenom-ena worthy of astonishment and admira-tion, but these were not of a type, which accorded with our understanding of sorce-ry and mysterious forces. There was for example a pair of birds, who were resid-ing since the beginning of winter in a re-cess near the cabin. Every morning they would wake us up with an intense patter-ing on the roof. After a while we were convinced, that they did this to demand their daily feed. This pair of birds, while looking like sparrows, were nearly as big as pigeons. They attracted our attention in particular, because on our first walk to the bus stop they escorted us there noisily. On our return from Inari in the late afternoon they accompanied us back to the cabin. This they repeated every week.

Incomprehensible as the behaviour of the birds appeared to us initially, in no time we got used to it and the many strange things, that seemed to be regular features of nature and culture in the region.

For the people here, especially for those, who lived in isolated cabins or in remote farmsteads close to the lakes and forests, in winter it was apparently the most natural thing in the world to provide the local wild animals, particularly the birds, with food. This practice had its roots in a different outlook to that, with which we in Germany associate the hanging out of suet cakes in the garden for birds or even with the feeding of deer and wild boars in the native forest districts and hunting grounds. We interpreted the behaviour of the people in Lapland as a more fundamental willingness to share resources and to close ranks in wintertime. We had the definite impression of a genuine respect on the part of the people living in the forest and lake regions towards their fellow creatures in the face of the devastatingly cold temperatures of the local winter. Without much consideration or even an attempt at imitation, such behaviour quickly became part of our daily routine also.

In the meanwhile, those three hours of twilight, in which we had to complete all important outside tasks, became the unit of measurement for dividing the days. The remaining period of darkness left us with more than enough time and opportunity, to pursue our original interests. With the aid of yogic concepts, science-based strategems and magical manoeuvers, I, for example, had spent several years questioning and challenging the recurring limits with regard to mental efficiency and physical control and in doing so had set new standards.

The interest, with which from an early age I had studied exotic religions and cultures as well as ancient knowledge and arts and attempted to understand the thinking and the secrets behind them, had grown to become more than just a hobby. Mere curiosity about untapped possibilities or promising discoveries was an inadequate explanation for my constant engagement with these spheres. Unquestioningly, a particular attraction lay for me in the fact of being able to draw upon a sheer endless repository of abandoned concepts, puerile riddles and impenetrable practices in the course of my efforts to critically question and stress test the thinking of modern science and culture as well as the axioms of current cosmology.

My endeavours and pursuits revolved ultimately around the question of power, its unleashing and the possibility for liberation. To this end I was determined to rebut all final justifications, concepts based upon the acceptance of fate and the adaptation to external forces along with the accompanying rationalisations and pseudo-successes, which for the most part are achieved at the expense of others. This uncompromising approach helped me to reach a high level of productiveness, experience amusing highpoints and extend my powers of communication. The pursuit of such a desire however leads to the hunger growing faster than its satiation. With the passing of time I succeeded in acquiring in those fields, which are supposedly the preserves of magic, religion and sorcery, extensive knowledge and a degree of proficiency. Nevertheless the display of such abilities, apart from being the product of deepest determination and intention, occasionally arose from practical speculation and the application of certain manoeuvers, free from rules, repetition and laws.

As might have been expected, I ended up amongst my friends with a reputation as an expert on anything and everything to do with magic and sorcery as well as for being able to draw upon a not inconsiderable practical competence. I can't deny, that the cachet, which went with having a reputation in these fields, lent added motivation to me, not to let up in my studies. Having said that, to date my fundamental attitude, which since back then has largely been shorn of such ulterior motives, has not changed in the slightest. This same attitude provided me with the material and the necessary tools for those corrections, which lie at the heart of my account under the all-encompassing title of "sorcery cold". In comparison with the frightening and ghastly experiences, which accompanied the start of this adventure and the turning point in my life, my earlier great insights and well-developed skills were no more than an ant's coughing in the midst of a thunderstorm.

In my pleasure-oriented youth I was, I must confess, somewhat conceited with regard to my supposed knowledge and abilities in the realm of magic and sorcery. This demeanour was undoubtely reinforced and encouraged in manifold ways by my social environment. This was perhaps, because people often like to play with fire and when things get out of control end up turning to the experts, be they actual or so-called, to rescue them from their predicaments. Having gladly and increasingly been called upon in such cases, my reputation as an expert in the area of magic was soon established. This development, however, contained its own dangerous dynamic, according to which the very memory of my original attitude with its incorruptible inklings was in danger of being lost.

In order to illustrate what I mean, I refer to an incident, which was spectacular for all involved and which took place during the first months of cohabitation with my then-girlfriend, Karin S.

In her flat-sharing community, where I was initially a guest and which I later joined, there lived a group of people with the most eclectic interests, nationalities and occupations. One of them, Frank, who was originally from Ghana and would soon become one of my most diligent karate students, would, in accordance with the mores of his native country, be visited regularly by friends, relatives and acquaintances from home. Before long, Karin and I were part of the "Ghanaian gang", many of whose members lived in the surrounding neighbourhood. In the course of the many ensuing encounters, mutual dinner invitations and social events, a particularly intense companionship developed between Seth, a distant relative of Frank's, Karin and me. Seth, who, like Frank, soon became a committed member of our karate group, used to visit us frequently, and on each occasion we found lots to talk about.

During one such discussion Seth revealed to me, that upon completing his education in Germany he intended returning to Ghana to become the apprentice of a witch-doctor, with whom he had made a solemn agreement prior to leaving Africa. In the course of the conversation Seth revealed a serious interest in the traditional arts and the ancient knowledge of his native country. Without prompting, he attempted to comfort me with the observation, that magical thinking was highly regarded and more respected in his country than was the case generally in Germany, which in the arrogance of the Enlightenment ran the risk of losing its cultural roots. For my part, I doubted, that such a loss was possible, as thus far I had been unable, despite the greatest of effort, to unearth any such roots in my own culture. On the basis of this and many other discussions it was clear, that Karin and I had established a more intimate and personal relationship with Seth than with any of his other compatriots.

When Frank didn't show up at our apartment for over a week, something which gave us cause for concern, we turned naturally to Seth for advice. He promised to be of prompt assistance, but then we didn't hear any more from him either. Late in the afternoon on one of the following days, I opened the door after much insistent knocking and ringing to find a Ghanaian, I had never seen before, standing in front of me. He bluntly informed me, that he was Frank's brother and would like to go to the latter's room, in order to fetch his belongings. I refused to let him in, declaring, that I hadn't the slightest proof of his identity and furthermore had no idea as to Frank's whereabouts. Sullenly, the man introduced himself as Isaac and insisted, that he was Frank's brother. He claimed, that Frank had been arrested by the police and was unable to come himself. I reprimanded Isaac, saying, that if this were the case, then it shouldn't be any problem for him to have power of attorney for Frank's belongings issued. Only then could we discuss his request, I stated. Furious and without saying as much as another word, Isaac turned on his heels and stormed down the stairs. I shouted after him, that he could make an appointment via telephone, as soon as he had the power of attorney.

When Karin heard about this episode, she told me, that she knew Isaac and that he had once behaved quite abusively and almost violently toward her. She asked me to deal with the matter, should he return.

The next time I opened the door for Isaac, he was neither unfriendly nor grumpy. I had to put my urge to immediately go mano-a-mano with him aside. He was in the company of a compatriot, who was the complete opposite of Frank's brother, if that's actually who was standing on the threshold. Isaac's companion was small, one metre sixty or sixty-five in height, wiry and outwardly restless and nervous. In comparison, Isaac was between one metre eighty-five and one metre ninety tall and appeared to be calmness personified. He handed over the power of attorney along with a letter of accreditation and a short note, in which Frank expressed his heartfelt thanks for everything and, as he was unlikely ever to be seen again, extended his farewells to everybody.

I showed the pair to Frank's room and let them get on with sorting his stuff and transporting it out of the apartment. All the while I sat between the corridor and the kitchen and casually observed them going about their task. The small wiry chap had something of the hobgoblin about him. Repeatly he attempted with short, sharp glances to catch my eye. I got the impression, that a strange tautness in his movement was supposed to draw attention to his dangerousness. As I didn't have my glasses on, I remained indifferent to the visual signals. I assume, that this circumstance led him to increase his efforts, but I remained for him an ungrateful audience, the more so as I was actually quite relaxed and relieved, that the whole process was being executed quickly and quietly.

This incident took place at the beginning of the week. Two days later, in other words midweek, sometime between ten and eleven in the evening, Karin burst, visibly shaken, into my new room - the very one, which Frank had just vacated and which I had begun arranging after my own fashion. Something had given her a terrible fright. She told me, that an invisible force in her room had twice shoved her violently and that the second time she had collided so heavily with the writing desk, that a lamp had been knocked over and broken. Without me to accompany her, she wasn't prepared to go back in there, she said.

So together we went into her room and did a quick tidying up. At that moment we decided not to indulge in fruitless speculation and cryptic discussion. Instead we treated ourselves to a quiet cup of tea, after which we intended to find peace and refuge in an early night's sleep.

After everything had settled down and we had been joined by a female flatmate, we found it easy to downplay and finally dismiss the whole matter. In the course of a lively discussion between Karin and the flatmate I enquired twice, if I could leave them to themselves for a quarter of an hour, in order to finish off a few things in my new room. Neither of them had a problem with that, so I went back to work.

After a short time I suddenly heard the two of them screaming. I reached the door to Karin's room, before the other members of the flat-sharing community had even managed to step into the corridor. Before speculation could develop, I had a plausible explanation ready: "A gigantic spider", I proclaimed loudly, while using sweeping gestures to express my own hopelessness. "Would anybody happen to have a jam jar or something similar?", I continued, as some of them returned to their rooms, shaking their heads, or head-ed for the toilet or the kitchen, in order to get out of the draft.

In a flash I was in the room with the two women. The flatmate, who was holding Karin tightly around the shoulders, appeared to be quite distraught. "This time it was a proper blow", said Karin through clenched teeth. Pia from the next room said merely: "I saw it." "Where?", I asked. "It looked like a strike to the face. Her head was knocked right back", pronounced Pia, who was trembling just as much as Karin. I hadn't the slightest idea, what might have happened. My curiosity, now aroused, started to take hold of me. Pia made her excuses and left the room. As she was going, I assured her, that I would keep an ear out in her direction and be with her immediately, should any emergency arise. Karin's jaw was lightly swollen and a bit of bruise was also visible. She indicated, that she could only speak with difficulty, and asked me not to leave. Together we finished putting my room to right in a quarter of an hour and decided, that this night, for once, we would be in bed by midnight. Having got the bed in the sleeping alcove ready, I had just stepped back into the main part of the room, where Karin was standing upright staring at the door to the corridor, when suddenly right in front of me she was whirled up into the air as if by a powerful jolt. Simultaneously she bent her upper body forward, before landing heavily on her feet, as if after a badly executed jump, thereby banging into the writing table for the second time in the one day. Not a word passed her lips. The wide-eyed expression alone indicated her shock at having just experienced something ghastly.

Immeasurable anger and ice cold curiosity were my dominant feelings at that moment. "Okay", I exclaimed in a threatening, martial tone of voice, only to follow it up softly with the words: "Want to try it on with someone else? Come on so." In saying this, I was filled by the deepest conviction, that anything, which was capable of grabbing hold of or attacking me, I could also grab hold of, attack and crush. Totally fired up, I stood for a moment. After a while Karin and I were left waiting, with nothing happening.

We headed to bed and under the shock of events were fast asleep in no time. No sooner had the light been turned off, than we started to forget all of what had happened. All of a sudden we were bathed in a bright light. I don't know, what was going on, but somehow the room was lit up, perhaps due to a light source outside. I awoke to find Karin pulling at my hair and turned to her immediately. She was sitting beside me with her back pressed against the wall.

Her eyes were wide open and she refused to let go of me.

When I looked in the direction Karin's eyes indicated, my heart nearly stopped there and then. At the very least I had to take a deep breath. Sitting against the wall opposite was a huge, fat Negro, who resembled a larger-than-life Sumo wrestler. He was wearing a series of necklaces made of the feathers and teeth of wild predators and his body was covered with war paint. Had the situation not been so absurd, due to the trustworthy expression on his face I would have considered him the friendliest person, I had ever seen. I felt like laughing and crying at the same time, but only managed to ask Karin, "Do you see ...?" "... the huge, fat Negro opposite?", she continued. At that, I shouted with all my might, while at the same time couldn't stop myself from laughing. I wanted to get to my feet, in order finally to engage with the eternally incomprehensible and fight it like a man. Before I could even make a move, the whole thing was over. Karin thanked me effusively and we were finally able to turn on the light. I wasn't remotely able to rationalise what had happened or put it in any kind of context. Neither the emerging thought, that we were dealing with a case of mass hysteria, nor the idea, that I had just experienced a border-line magical episode or even something supernatural, seemed conclusive to me. An aversion to any kind of speculation happened to be one of my personality traits. Whenever one or other difficult situation in my social environment resolved itself in a manner, that was not disadvantageous to me, it appeared more logical to many of my friends and persons, who were involved, than to my own mind. Despite my growing interest in the incomprehensible and the impossible, back then I hadn't yet left the fatal inclination, not to eschew short-term social advantages, behind me. Like many people in my circle of friends I too was at times convinced - to the point of willfulness and beyond - of my magical abilities and knowledge.

Similarly, the words, which Seth later said to me, were fuel to the fire of my own pretentions. On enquiry, about three weeks later, he explained to us, that Isaac had hired a sorcerer, who had a sinister and credible reputation, in order firstly to protect himself from me and Karin and secondly to harm and injure us seriously. My description of the small, sinewy fellow was enough for Seth to confirm, that we had encountered said sorcerer. Frank, he told us further, had been detained by the immigration police and expelled from Germany, while Isaac hadn't been seen for a couple of days and seemed to have disappeared without a trace along with the infamous witch doctor. Seth dismissed our assumption, that Isaac had returned to Ghana to be with his brother, with a cynical facial expression. According to him, Frank wasn't Isaac's brother at all and had no reason to voluntarily give up his good job as an automobile technician in a large garage. Furthermore the two of them came from the same village and there no one had heard from him for a while.

*

While going about the daily chores in our winter retreat in Lapland, there were moments, when boredom, intellectual arrogance and the presumption of my own eminent qualifications for dealing with and mastering the unknown would have me doubting the suitability of the location and the circumstances of the situation. Whenever this occurred, my unrelenting instinct and an undying premonition would sober me up and liberate and redirect my attention uncompromisingly toward the next step.

At that time I wasn't aware, that on the basis of my previous experiences and adventures, a dangerous and deceptive conceit had developed within me, which under the shock of its obliteration via the encounter with irrefutable forces was soon to come to a painful end - and me nearly along with it, had I been completely attached to it.

Lapland
(Part 3)

From the vantage point of the present the claim, that decisive events cast their shadow ahead, always sounds a little contrived. However, the first serious impression on the morning of our shopping visit to Inari, namely that our avian neighbours hadn't showed up for their daily feeding, caused us to worry and speculate. Moments later, as we glanced back at the cabin from a distance of about 150 metres, we were confronted with a vision, from which we were unable to tear our eyes.

An inordinately large crow- or raven-like bird was sitting, pitch-black and motionless as a statue, on the edge of the cabin roof. I can't even begin to describe the sensory confusion, which the presence of such a large black bird in front of a snow-covered background could cause in the beholder. To make things worse, it was also the creature's strange size, which inexorably impeded the natural reaction to compare or examine it for further recognisable features.

Our usual Monday companions on the other hand were nowhere to be seen. It was only after we had been staring for a while, that we noticed, how still everything was.

Having got going again, so that we wouldn't miss our connection with the bus on the northern highway, both of us were caught up the whole way in our own private fantasies. It was only much later, that we spoke about the apparition of the large black bird and the various impressions, we associated with it.

As the months progressed, the fading light became more diffuse, spreading itself ever thinly across the horizon. The cloud formations reminded us of the stormy, wet weather we were used to on the North Sea coast in the autumn, without the wind and the rain. The disappearing daybreak was reflected in the snow and ice.

Having briskly completed our weekly shopping, we went to the bari for tea and coffee. Sitting there beside the entrance to the bari, we passed the time watching the people outside through the display window, which afforded a perfect view of everything happening on the village's main open space. The ground was covered with ice and as voyeurs in the cozy warmth of the bari, we allowed ourselves to be entertained by the clumsy efforts of the locals to traverse the slippy surface.

Along with ourselves there were four other people in the saloon, among them, as ever, the man, whom two weeks previously I had dared to ask about the local shamans. As we had found out, a discussion of that nature was indicative in these parts of a close acquaintance. For that reason, he and I had already acknowledged each other's presence with a polite nod. Although we were the tourists, everything appeared so familiar, that we felt practically, as if we already belonged to the Monday lunch-time regulars in the bari in Inari.

Meanwhile, our attention had been drawn to a group of children and teenagers on the icy square, who were having fun, sliding over and back, shoving one another and carrying out risky manoeuvers on the slippery surface. All of a sudden, the kids scattered in all directions. Apparently they were as startled as ourselves by the appearance of a Sami, who, having just entered the square, had poised for a moment and was turning his head quickly from side to side, as if he was trying to pick up a scent. He had to be a Sami, as he was dressed from head to toe in a traditional costume, which I, incorrectly, due to a lack of knowledge, took for the local garb. His conspicuous lack of height was starkly emphasised by his long frizzy hair, which stood out wildly from his head and gave him the look of a dangerous predator. His clothes, black like his hair, were, in accordance with the local traditions, covered with sown-on patches of different patterns and colours, including blue, red and white. In contrast, however, to the other Sami in their traditional garb, he didn't wear a cap or a many-pointed hat. His hair probably wouldn't have allowed it.

At any rate, there wasn't much time to examine his appearance, as with haste and determination he had set off again. Over the ice he ran - or rather rolled and slid - as quick as a snowmobile in the direction of the door of the bari. Our eyes were so transfixed by this apparition and its incomparably quick and ominously coherent movements, that it took the sound of footsteps and stools falling over to remind us of where we were - in the cafe.

With a fright we noticed, that the four men, who like ourselves had been in the bari only moments before, had taken flight and were attempting to leave as quickly as possible by the back entrance on the other side of the room. The proprietor, the only other person remaining, had taken cover behind the counter. Before we knew what was happening, the front door burst open and this unusual human bundle of energy stood for a short moment in the middle of the room. With his hair, arms and legs he exuded an undeniable physical-spacial presence. It looked, as if he was trying to get his bearings. And then he turned his face in our direction.

In that moment I was overcome by a terrible shock, because despite all curiosity, effort and intent, I couldn't for the life of me make out his face or his eyes, even though they were the very things I was trying to find with my gaze. Whenever I later tried to remember, what exactly it was, that I had seen, or whenever I struggled to recall the face of this strange person, all that I was left with was the memory of an old, wrinkled and nondescript piece of leather.

Before I knew it, he had advanced eight metres to the counter. There, standing on the footrail, he reached behind the counter, extended his arm like a fishing rod and pulled forth the bar keeper. His movements were so fast, it was like looking at a still image. We looked on, as the little Sami dragged the man, who we knew as the bar keeper, along behind him. The latter, with his whole body trembling and seemingly resigned to his fate, trotted along behind the giant bumblebee.

As if nothing had happened, the three regular guests returned and took up their places in the warm saloon. The bar keeper or whoever he was and the little man didn't reappear. I looked over to the neighboring table, where the guy, from whom we had previously made enquiries, was sitting, imbibing some kind of hot drink. As he didn't look away, I decided to ask him about what had happened, well knowing that perhaps he wouldn't be able to understand me very well. "So tell us, was that a member of the local heritage group?", I enquired. He beckoned us over to his table and then, to our surprise, began to whisper in German: "This is all very embarrassing for us. I must apologise, as the person, you have just seen, would at an earlier period in our culture have been described as a shaman. In all honesty, I say to you, that no one hereabouts would dream about admitting his existence to strangers. Even among ourselves nobody talks about it. It's taboo." Everything he knew about this person was ill-boding and not a subject for polite conversation among Christians. Having just seen for ourselves at close range the man in action, it was clear, that all the sinister machinations and unusual abilities ascribed to such persons simply had to be true.

In the course of his explanation my interlocutor began to realise, that instead of cooling my curiosity he had inflamed it. Just as I started to ask him, if he could possibly tell me, where ... he interrupted me curtly and forcefully. "No. I'm not saying anymore about it. And you can be sure, that nobody here will help you in any way either", he declaimed with a sweeping gesture of his hand. He pointed out, that the man had no address or fixed abode, at which he could be reached. Apparently he truly lived, as if back in the prehistoric age.

I was able to temper the bari patron's uneasiness somewhat, by emphatically promising to take his advice and thanking him profusely for his honesty. For his part, he assuaged our consternation at the fact of suddenly being able to communicate with him in German with the explanation, that he, like many of his older compatriots, who were fluent in our language, had since the Second World War developed a deep aversion to using it.

On this afternoon we parted as neighbours. The breezy resoluteness, which made it easy for me to leave our interlocutor with a good impression, was due of course to completely opposite reasons.

On the long way back to the cabin Kirsten and I agreed, that we each in our own way had experienced and observed the same things. Both of us were filled with an inner certitude, that in our search for an authentic and irrefutable magical tradition we had just stumbled across the first indications of its existence. Travelling back from Inari it was clear to us, that we had come to the right place. It seemed eminently logical, that the attainment of the type of knowledge, we were seeking, wouldn't correspond to the normal sequences or steps of initia-

tion, which apply in conventional learn-
ing situations.

As we reached the cabin, it was too dark
for us to be on the lookout for anything.

Lapland
(Part 4)

A fire to warm ourselves up, a little bite to eat in the late evening and a hot mug of tea along with an absorbing book to read were the things we used to create a cozy atmosphere in the cabin at the end of each shopping Monday. On this particular evening, however, the stillness of the surrounding forest with its powdery snow covering seemed to extend as far as our open fireplace. In light of the long day we'd had, we decided to head to bed at about ten o'clock. While there were still embers burning in the fireplace, we were determined to trap as much of our body heat as well as of the room temperature underneath the two woolen blankets, we both had, for as long as possible. As the fire slowly died out and with our thoughts still racing like mad, we dosed off slowly towards the land of nod and a deep sleep.

Awakened by a sudden blast of icy cold air on my back, I reluctantly opened my eyes to discover, that I must have turned over in my sleep, as I was facing the wooden cabin wall, upon which the last flickers of light from the embers were performing a shadowy dance. As I looked around to ascertain the source of cold-ness, incomprehensibility to the point of confusion immobilised me for a couple of seconds, as the front door of the cabin was wide open. My bed lay along the wall opposite the front door, which, be-fore retiring to bed, we used to double lock. For additional insulation we also used to hang a heavy blanket, which we had found in the small basement under-neath the cabin, over the doorframe. This improvised curtain created be-tween itself and the door an air pocket, which helped to keep the cold out. In this instance, however, the blanket was drawn to one side and the wide open door was swaying gently in the wind. Af-ter a short moment of numbness l leapt out of bed and reached the door in an in-stant. Ignoring the dark tranquility out-side, I grabbed for the latch and slam-med the door shut. In my rush to lock it as tightly and as quickly as possible, I ended up getting somewhat confused.

I was still putting the curtain back in place, when Kirsten asked me, what was going on. I asked her to give me a hand and somewhat ungraciously she acceded to my request. She enquired, where all the snow and slush on the floor of the cabin had come from, and I told her the little I knew. In silence we mopped up the watery mess and crawled back under our woolen blankets. The embers of the fire were no longer to be seen and the stillness outside seemed to penetrate even the slightest cracks in the cabin walls.

The next morning at breakfast time our bird companions didn't show up for their feed. Apart from that we couldn't find anything in particular, which might nourish our suspicions. It wasn't until later the following evening, as we were settling down to have a relaxing read, that we suddenly heard a heavy thump on the roof of the cabin. We both thought immediately of the large black bird, which we had observed two days earlier on the roof, and began to make conjectures. Even if it was the very same large black bird, whose landing on the roof we assumed we had just heard, neither of us was in any way inclined to go outside to check. Having yet again managed to mislay our torches, we were reliant on a petroleum lamp. It seemed pointless to try and discern anything with its weak light.

It was with a sense of disquiet, that we again headed off earlier than usual to bed, while striving at the same time to keep an eye on the door and the windows.

In the middle of the night I awoke, feeling as if I hadn't slept a wink. The fire was long gone out and there were no reflections of the embers to be seen anywhere. By the murky, pale light of the moon the familiar objects in the room were still visible. Not everything in my immediate surroundings was familiar, I realised with a shock, as slowly a form appeared from behind the curtain over the closed door. With a quick glance in the direction of the other bed, I was able to rule out the possibility, that it was merely Kirsten moving around. With short muffled shouts I tried to waken her, but to no avail.

Confronted with the irrefutable threat of my own extermination by a merciless force, I became mentally and physically aware of just how futile the attempt to feign paying the price of death by recourse to archaic panic with its accompanying sensations of confinement and numbness can prove in the end to be. I was overcome by the sudden and acute realisation, that this shadow, which in the meantime had reached the middle of the cabin, embodied the one thing, which in my life I never wanted to encounter. The only direction available to me was backwards and so I pressed my body against the cabin wall, as if trying to push out the beams.

As a result, I failed to notice, that the shadow, whose outline, disturbingly, was becoming ever easier to make out, had paused in the middle of the cabin. It seemed, as if a complex pressure, composed of danger, threat and total distress, was bearing relentlessly down upon me. Animals fleeing before a wildfire in the savannah must feel as I did in that moment. With my back I could make out the crack between the beams and the cold air forcing its way through there so clearly, that I fancied I might just fuse myself with its coldness and let it suck me out in an icy maelstrom away from the strait, in which I found myself.

I was increasingly unable to tell, which was the greater threat: the shadowy figure in the centre of the cabin, which I thought I recognised as the little man, of whom the locals were all so obviously afraid, or the coldness in the splits and cracks of the wooden wall, which was only prevented from sucking me out of the cabin completely by the wind, which was blowing steadily against the outside of our dwelling. Incapable of emitting even the slightest sound, I slowly came to the conclusion, that I was dealing with the mysterious person, or whatever it was, whose face I had been unable to make out or withstand in the bari in Inari.

Like a lock snapping shut, in my moment of certainty the little man raised his arm in my direction. In response to my own panic-stricken attempt at retreat, it seemed to grow to three times its original length. Suddenly this hand grabbed my arm and - I cannot describe it any other way - ripped me with superhuman force out of the cracks in the wooden wall and back into the cabin. Due to the speed and the energy, with which this ensued, I was catapulted out of my bed and crashed heavily onto the floor. Never turning my eyes away from the man, I saw, that the reason for the extension of his arm was a strangely shaped club, which he held in his hand. Despite the appallingly poor light conditions, I was able to make out a stick, which tapered off like an archaic walking staff conically in the direction of his hand and which had at its raised end a thick knob. At the same time it was too slender to be a club and too short to be a walking stick. With what then, for goodness sake, had this strange little man, whose face remained in the shadows, grabbed hold of me?

I was completely under the spell of the raised club. Its outline would remain etched in my memory, due to the impression, that it was about to execute its murderous function on me. For this reason, I didn't initially notice, that the little man's form had begun to shrink. It happened so fast, that by the time it became irreversible, no opportunity for the slightest reflection or thought remained. I was simply compelled to look on, as his form shrunk to a sinister tad the size of a fist, before moving ponderously in the direction of the fireplace and disappearing into it.

I almost failed to notice the fluttering and banging of large wings on the roof of the cabin. With my whole body shaking, I summoned what was left of my senses, reached for the matches and, after about two minutes of staggering around, finally lit a candle.

Kirsten slept on, as if anaesthetised. The improvised cross, which I had made the day before out of pipe cleaners and, in accordance with my Christian upbringing, intuitively hung for protection over my bed, lay ripped to little pieces all over the floor of the cabin.

Shortly afterwards, yet long before daybreak, Kirsten and I sat at the table in the light of the candle and the fire. After drinking half a cup of tea, Kirsten finally found her voice and said: "I had a terrible dream last night."

The Northern Lights
(Part 1)

It was snowing heavily. We were standing outside the door of our cabin, just about to depart, when it struck me, that since the onset of deepest winter we hadn't experienced this amount of snowfall. Nevertheless, we weren't going to allow ourselves to be prevented from going for a walk by the curtain of snow or the remaining two and half hours of faint daylight. After that recent terrible and frightening night, the after-effects of which we could still feel, we had once before postponed our planned excursion. Today, however, we were certain, that the conditions couldn't be better nor the opportunity more auspicious. We were heading off on our first and perhaps last unconstrained exploration of the vicinity of our cabin. Under the pertaining weather and light conditions a more ambitious or extensive expedition was not possible.

Like all the actual or imagined trails in these forests, the path we took could not simply be identified on the basis of external features as a well-trodden mud track, but rather had to be discovered by our feet on the basis of its walkability.

With our good sense of balance, sure-footedness and determination to penetrate as far as possible into the forest, we were able to make good progress. Occasionally we had to retrace our steps over stretches of differing length, in order to get around a hill, which we perhaps hadn't seen in time, or a patch of marshy ground, on to which we had trodden inadvertently. With our heads bent over, scanning the ground ahead of us, we kept up a decent pace. In order to avoid becoming separated from one another, we exchanged words frequently. After a while I began to question, what it was we were hoping to achieve with our little walkabout. In comparison to the area surrounding the lake with its smaller coniferous and birch trees, out here in the depths of the forest there was nothing to be seen other than countless large pines, which blocked the view of the surrounding countryside.

Gradually the soundscape changed and slowly took us under its spell. Subterranean wells and rivers, which were coursing through the scree of the rocky, hollow ground under our feet and alongside the path, were burbling and gurgling with such variety, that it was like listening to an aquatic orchestra. Somewhere in the distance sounds like rusty, old castle doors creaking and squeaking on their hinges could be heard. Later, we discovered the source was a grove of extremely large, dead and decaying pine trees, whose split trunks were collaborating with the constant wind to create this eerie noise.

I found the creaking and squeaking, the gurgling und burbling all somewhat unsettling. My imagination was already running wild and I had no desire to experience an unpleasant surprise again. A branch of wood with the girth of a human thigh was blocking the hidden path, which we could sense ever better beneath our feet. Just as I was about to pick this seemingly dead piece of wood up and clear it out of our way, I noticed, that it was actually alive. It was the out-growth of an old and majestic pine tree and crossed our path at a height of about twenty centimetres. The obvious question, as to why our path led directly under this low-hanging branch, conjured up straight away in my mind visions of dark caves and chuckling, noisily eating trolls, who surely inhabited the rocky, hollow underground.

The sound of old, creaking castle doors, which had seemed totally out of place in these surroundings, acquired all of sudden a degree of plausibility. Nevertheless, in the context of the events, which were yet to come, this image would later be revealed to be nothing more than a pleasant and fairytale-like fantasy.

After clambering over the branch and, like as if in an adventure park, advancing another twenty paces further along, I came upon an object, which immediately caught my interest. I crouched down, only to find myself confronted with something, which I would have preferred not to see in this place nor have to try and rationalise. Somehow, I had managed to stumble across a large bone, a shoulder blade to be exact, which was bloody and from which flesh was still hanging.

"Kirsten!", I called out, while simultaneously striving to keep my composure. In no time, she was standing beside me, straining her eyes in the twilight to make out my terrible discovery. In an attempt to establish the origin of the bloody bone, I leapt up instinctively and advanced a couple of steps forward with my gaze fixed on the ground. It was

Kirsten, who discovered the next bone. Before long we had found so many bones spread out over the small clearing, that we slowly started getting worried. Many of them were merely gnawed and all around splatterings of blood could be seen. Depite our restricted field of vision, after searching an area of about thirty square metres we were convinced, that we knew what had happened. Some animal, a reindeer perhaps, had met a bitter end here - torn apart and partially devoured by a horde of predators.

Without exchanging words, we were in total agreement, that we had to get away from this place and back to our cabin as quickly as possible. Under the circumstances, I reckoned a stick or a rock might come in handy. Again, without speaking and with the same thing in mind, Kirsten and I began searching the immediate surroundings for something we could use to defend ourselves with. As the temperature was about twenty-five degrees celsius below zero, it wasn't simply possible to detach a stone from the ground, and in the poor light, with everything covered in thick snow, a stick or a suitable branch was hard to come across.

Despite being in a hurry and with a visibility of not more than a metre, we were preoccupied with finding something with which to arm ourselves. Feeling somewhat under stress and a little bit desperate, without taking my gloves off I fumbled with one hand over the edge of a boulder, while using the other one to support myself against the huge stone. If it were wolves, we were dealing with, a cudgel wouldn't be of much use, I thought to myself, as I shoved my hand ever further beyond the edge of the rock.

Suddenly, without the slightest warning, something grabbed hold of my wrist. "So you also reckon, that we're most likely to find a piece of wood here?", I asked Kirsten, under the assumption, that it was she on the other side of the boulder. I was just about to ask her to let go, when I heard her calling out to me from a distance of about fifteen metres, asking me to repeat myself, as she hadn't heard me properly.

I don't recall, what I did first: shout or jump up and jerk my arm. At any rate, my feeling of panic grew exponentially, because whatever was gripping my hand wouldn't let go. Before I knew it, Kirsten was at my side. With a strong slap to the face she brought me to my senses. I no longer had the feeling of being held. In its place I held something in my hand, which turned out to be less of a stick and more a long wooden root, resembling a club. An urge, composed of inner tension and playful instinct, caused me suddenly to strike the large rock twice with this root, using all the power I could muster. Upon the first blow the front end of the root was left hanging off and with the second one it fell to the ground. Kirsten stooped and picked it up in her hands, as if it were some kind of tool. Sticking close together, we made our way back to the cabin.

In hindsight, I'm of the opinion, that we were very fortunate, despite bad weather and near darkness, to find our way back unharmed. Perhaps it was also due to the fact, that we had stopped relying on our visual sense of orientation and instead just let our feet guide us.

On the walk back I held the strange root segment up close to my face repeatedly, in order to get a sense of what it reminded me. It is for that reason, that I, upon getting within view of the cabin and being fairly sure, that there were no wolves trailing us, threw this clublike object with all my might back into the forest in the direction, from which we had come. Kirsten, in contrast, brought her piece of the root with her into the cabin. Amazingly, we slept deeply and soundly that night.

Being aware, that the locals let their reindeers graze freely in the woods nearby, and also to reassure ourselves, we set off the next morning on foot to Talvitupa, in order to leave a message for the owner of our cabin, requesting, that he pay us a visit as soon as possible. I have no idea, whether our communication was passed on by telephone or by some other method. Whichever it was, we had hardly completed the trail back from the Northern Highway to our cabin, when the landlord arrived in his car.

With the help of a dictionary and by resorting to all sorts of gesticulations, we managed in the shortest possible time to describe to him, what we had discovered early the previous afternoon. We made a great effort to convey to him our concern, that wolves could have been involved. For his part, our landlord did all in his power to convince us, that we had nothing to worry about. He pointed out, that no wolves had crossed the border from Russia for many years. This led him to dismiss the possibility, that they were responsible for what had occurred.

As we struggled to make ourselves mutually understood, the landlord, who, as the owner of a sawmill was used to dealing daily with every shape, size and state of wood, did something quite remarkable and surprising. Out of curiosity, he picked up the broken piece of root, which Kirsten upon our return the previous evening hadn't put away but rather left directly beside the fireplace. He raised it up towards the window and examined it with such calmness and solemnity, that Kirsten and I both fell into a silent reverie. Suddenly, as if there was nothing more important for us to talk about, he held the piece of wood in front of our faces, repeating fervidly again and again the word "revontulet". It was, as if, with this single utterance he was articulating everything, which could be said in the situation about this wooden fragment.

Eventually, he put the broken piece of root back carefully where he had found it and smilingly declared with a degree of finality: "Revontulet". With the one arm outstretched, he indicated in the direction of the window, and with the other hand he pointed by turns at the fireplace and the cabin ceiling. In the face of such certitude, we could nothing other than nod in agreement and with understanding.

It was only after our visitor had departed, that we dared to consult the dictionary. Initially, this only added to our puzzlement. We reached for the object, which had caused our landlord such obvious joy and led to his immense outburst, in order to examine it ourselves more closely. After washing it with water and removing all the leftover bits of clay and dirt, we held it up to the light of day. It shone so brightly, that the realisation came over us. In the nearly white woodgrain we were able to discern in fine detail a flickering tongue of flame, which, with its various shades of red and yellow, reminded us of the flashing, roaming light show we had been able to experience for the first time for ourselves in the skies of this region.

There was no doubt about it. The man had been referring to the Northern Lights.

Northern Lights
(Part 2)

The eerie phenomena and a growing sense of doom, which cast long shadows over our temporary living circumstances, must nonetheless be clearly differentiated from the harassments and the primeval fear, which an unsolicited encounter with the real masters, hunters and predators of this area can call forth from the realm of elementals and shamans.

A day and a half after the thought-provoking conversation about the Northern Lights, we met our landlord again. He was standing in front of our cabin with a group of the neighbours, who were engaged in a loud and disharmonious discussion. Although all of them were armed with hunting rifles and clubs, they seemed nervous and somewhat disorganised. Certainly, during all our time in Inari I never saw so many cars as on this particular morning.

Out of consideration for his hunting companions, the landlord enquired of us with a degree of reservation about the location, where we had come across the dead reindeer. He lowered his voice, as he asked us conspiratorially: "Wolves, where...?" In doing so, he indicated with his hand the outline of a semicircle above the treetops in front of us. In response to the earnest look on my face and my repeating his question with feigned horror, he shook his head vigourously and insisted, that we had nothing to worry about. After we had explained the route by means of non-verbal gestures and a drawing in the snow, the group headed off quickly with a silent farewell and soon had disappeared into the forest. As we ourselves had been just about to set off for Inari to do some shopping, we were now in a quite a hurry to reach the Northern Highway in time, so as not to miss our bus.

This meeting only served to heighten our inner tensions and sharpen our attentiveness. Nonetheless, on the entire trip to and from Inari we didn't observe anything out of the ordinary or glimpse anything strange out of the corners of our eyes. To our dismay however, we did notice, that only one of the two birds, who regularly accompanied us to the Northern Highway and back, joined us this afternoon on return to the cabin.

On this particular day, it appeared, that there were to be no more surprises, which might interrupt the routine chores. Almost imperceptively afternoon was followed by early night, until eventually, with no little satisfaction, we took our thoughts and dreams with us to the welcoming bed.

All of a sudden, we were shook out of our peaceful slumber by loud, scratching noises. The sounds of scraping, branches cracking and the pattering of feet couldn't be ignored, as they were coming from right outside of the cabin. These noises were in total contrast to the silence, which predominates in these parts. As such, it would have been humanly impossible to sleep through them by integrating them into one's dreams. All the tensions of the previous day were laid bare again.

Armed with one of the torches, which in the meantime had turned up again, and with some trepidation I made my way over to the door. In order to stay calm, I engaged Kirsten in a one-sided conversation, during which I described what I was up to and what I intended to do in the next moment.

On opening the door I found myself facing numerous radiant pairs of eyes. The last thing I would have expected to come across in the middle of the night was an assembly of highly alert forest denizens. With a fright, I slammed the door shut as hard as I could and locked it, turning the key in the lock as far as it would go.

Kirsten, who by now was awake, stood at my side. That gave me the courage to open the door again, despite all the sounds outside, which could still be heard clearly. Having by this stage composed ourselves, we approached the situation with care and began to illuminate the area in front of the door systematically. The disturbers of the nocturnal peace turned out to be nothing more than a small herd of reindeer, who were treating themselves to the bark of the trees and the marsh grass around our cabin. We surmised, that these reindeers were used to interacting with humans and were therefore highly relieved, that it wasn't wolves we had to cope with out here on our own in the middle of nowhere.

After returning to bed, we couldn't get back to sleep for a long while. As a result, we were both pretty tired the next morning. We cooked ourselves a delicious breakfast and that got us back on our feet.

In our splendid isolation, far removed from other human settlements, any unexpected encounter with animals or strangers was for all participants a mix of suspense, fear and aggression. Later, providing the usual rituals of getting to know one another had been observed, this gave way to a combination of elegant restraint and careful receptivity. Encounters with humans and animals in the wild, even at a distance, regularly took on the character of a little adventure, to a degree, which, under the usual circumstances of civilisation, one would not have imagined possible. Due to the possibility of unforeseen events and unpredictable deviations from the normal run of things our attentiveness was kept more aroused, than we would have been used to in our everyday lives in Germany. In this context, a steady and growing interest for everything and anything in the immediate vicinity of our lodgings became for us second nature.

It was for this very reason, that at night Kirsten and I would visit the outhouse together, which was situated about fifty metres away from the cabin in a storage shed for wood and equipment. The prevailing darkness, which prevented one from seeing one's hand in front of one's face, made the outhouse an unsafe and spooky place.

While taking turns using the toilet, we used to maintain contact and assure each other of our presence, by keeping a conversation going. On one particular occasion, however, something quite strange happened, which, in association with fear, wariness and hideous fantasies, we haven't to this day been able to explain fully. As such, it has been filed away as one of those unexpected incidents, which invariably result from a chain of unfortunate events.

While sitting on the privy, a brief interruption in the flow of conversation triggered terrible visions in my mind. It was obvious, that if someone wanted to carry out an ambush, this was the perfect opportunity. In order to separate myself and Kirsten, all the attacker had to do was to lock the outhouse door from outside, and he or she would be in control of the situation.

Before I knew it, these negative feelings had congealed into an internal cramp. On my fifth attempt at calling out to Kirsten on the other side of the shed, I was yet again left futily waiting for an answer. Each shout was met with silence, which went on for seconds. My thoughts careered back and forth between hope and fear. "Surely something untoward could never happen to us at night out here in the wilderness", I rationalised. As my patience finally reached its limit, I tested the door of the outhouse, only to find that it had, in fact, been latched from the outside.

In that moment, I felt as if the shock was about to split my chest wide open. The time for hesitation and reflection was over. Blind to any potential injury, I took two and half steps back from the door, threw myself against it with all my force and landed with a crash on my face on the ground outside.

I jumped straight to my feet and called out into the darkness, but Kirsten was nowhere to be seen or heard. Filled by a dark foreboding, while simultaneously attempting to make light of the situation, I spun around and ran angrily along the track towards the cabin, through the open door of which the bright light of the fire could be seen. On entering the cabin, I found Kirsten sitting in front of the fireplace with a mug of tea in her hand, as if nothing in the world could discommode her. I had no reason to doubt in the slightest her statement, made with astonishment and conviction, that she hadn't the slightest idea, how she had gotten back there. Although we later spoke often about this incident, we never were able to work out, what actually had happened in those couple of minutes between the cabin and the shed.

This and similar episodes, which from our perspective didn't seem inappropriate to the foreign surroundings, kept us very much on our toes, when going about even the most minor of tasks. In no way, however, should these impressions and experiences be even remotely confused with the unexplainable, unavoidable and frightening attacks, which since our encounter with Leatherface - this being the name I had decided to use for the unmentionable local shaman - in the bari in Inari were imposing themselves ever more frequently and with increasingly destructive force on our attempts to maintain a semblance of normality.

As we would soon come to understand, each and every one of these attacks and intrusions had a compelling common feature. For me, all of them harked back to my earlier, instinctive decision to throw the weird piece of wood, which, at the place, where we found the dead reindeer, had undoubtedly reached out to me, as far as I could and with all my might blindly back into the forest. These incidents had, in their entirety, somehow began with Leatherface and the fire on the island, which originally wouldn't light. The enduring certitude, with which the encounter with the strange Norwegian in Hamburg and his curious way of looking at the plaster relief, had left me, had, in the meantime, evolved into a kind of leitmotif, which was starting to provide explanations for and an understanding of the ongoing adventures.

Such an inner calling can find its expression in a freedom of movement. For someone, who has acquired the ability to read and decipher the corresponding signs, it manifests itself in the certitude, that over and above the individual's daily struggle for survival, compounded by rumours, stories and hyperbole, there are greater and more important things to learn and to do than to worry about social recognition or one's own personal well-being.

As I have alluded to with a couple of examples, Kirsten and I were already quite versed in handling the sudden emergence of strange phenomena or un-expected incidents. I must, however, em-phasise, that nothing we had previously experienced bore the slightest compari-son with the episodes, which I would ascribe to a fateful wave of encounters and attacks, which, taking place without exception in Finnish Lapland, had taken on an inexorable, irresistable legacy, whose ultimate implications are to this day unclear.

It must have been about three days after the events surrounding our discovery of the reindeer cadaver, that Kirsten and I were again suddenly woken up in the middle of the night by a deafening noise. It sounded, as if someone had put every piece of cutlery they could find in a cook-ing pot and were trying to see just how much noise they could make by banging and grinding the various knives, forks and spoons against the metal insides of their improvised sound instrument.

The racket was clearly coming from the cabin's kitchenette. My initial presumption, that the cause had to be a mouse, which had become trapped in a pot full of cutlery, was dispelled by Kirsten, who, having gone with the torch to check, was now suggesting, that I should come and have a look for myself.

The noise continued unbroken, as I stood beside her and in the weak beam of the torch saw something, which under other circumstances wouldn't have even rated as a practical joke, because it looked so stupid and easy, while at the same time seemingly impossible.

The pot wasn't resting on anything, but rather was hanging in the air at waist height and being continuously shaken by an unseen hand. Other than that, there was nothing particularly strange or threatening about it. Neither our cries for help and nor our hurried prayers had any effect on what we were seeing and hearing. Something was shaking the pot wildly back and forth. As it was at waist height, we were able to see into it, but nowhere could we detect a mouse or anything else, which might have made the proceedings understandable.

A moment of horror and a simultaneous paralysis of my entire body seemed to stretch into infinity. Kirsten, acting on a spontaneous impulse, reached around the corner to the fireplace, grabbed the broken piece of wood with the image of the Northern Lights in it and flung it at the cooking pot. Immediately it fell to the ground and normal stillness resumed. We concurred, that no more than half a minute had passed, since we had been woken up by the clatter of cutlery and pot.

It was that same week, late one afternoon, as darkness was starting to overtake twilight, that I, having completed my daily chores, took a little stroll down the track in the direction we had gone on our one and only unconstrained exploration of the surrounding forest and thereby stumbled across the reindeer remains. After only a few metres I stopped, undecided, as if standing before a threshold, and looked up along the barely identifiable trail, which wound its way past hollows, little knolls and giant rocks of the forest. In vain my eyes repeatedly tried to make out the course of the path, only each time to lose track of it after only a few metres.

Seemingly out of nowhere, I was hit by a loud and heavy blow to the back. The force of it was so great, that I was knocked to the ground, landing on my face and stomach. I was overcome by a pain so great, that I instinctively drew my limbs in towards my torso, so as not to black out. It was only after I was able to distinguish the pain of the blow to my back from those in my knees and elbows, which I had incurred, when crashing to the ground, that I was seized by a sense of inner distress, the like of which I had never before known and which brought my mind back to the trail. After taking a couple of steps, I stood for a moment and looked around. There, where only moments before I had stood and been knocked to the ground, roughly thirty metres from my current, seemingly safe vantage point, a large and heavy branch was to be seen at a height of about half a metre above the trail. Jutting out of the pine trees, with the twilight in the background, it exuded a vitality and a massivity, as if it had always been there.

I was filled with an uncertainty, which only made the pain in my back and my sense of dread worse. In order to calm myself down, I shook my head vigorously and beat a retreat to the nearby cabin.

Kirsten already had the tea going on the stove, and the warmth from inside and outside allowed me to slip into brief forgetfulness.

The following week, on our shopping trip to Inari, we were walking, hale and hearty, in the diffused late morning light, along our well-trodden path through the forest to the bus stop. Every now and again our wandering gaze would rest upon the surrounding, long-drawn out hillocks and ridges, which, at a height of between 100 and 300 metres, interrupted the line of the horizon.

The heighest chain of hills, which could be seen from about half way along the trail, regularly drew our attention. Of all the visual attractions for some reason it excited our curiosity the most. Once a week we were able to feast our eyes on these beautiful mountains, which, like giant craggy walls, reinforced by ice and snow, jutted out of the surrounding forest landscape, as if they had just emerged.

At this stage we were familiar with the highest peak of around 300 metres, as if it were a long lost friend. Having often-times on our way to the bus stop examined it from a distance, we had become acquainted with many of its features. It was for that reason, that we again stood to admire it with wonder and awe. This time, however, something seemed amiss. The front slope of the hill, which usually was as easy to survey as a map, lay hidden behind a jet black shadow, which extended all the way up to the summit. None of the contours of the little mountain were to be discerned. Only the highest ridge could be made out against the morning twilight, which was breaking over it into the surrounding landscape of rocks, snow and trees. With its indescribable eerieness the shadow had something compelling about it. After a couple of minutes we set off again, straying, however, steadily from our original path. As if wanting to explore a mystery, we were slowly but surely heading ever more in the direction of the hill, which lay a little bit beyond and to the left of the trail to the Northern Highway. In hindsight, it would appear, that the shadow was drawing us magically towards it.

We must have been walking for quite a while, before we noticed, that the shadow on the front slope of the little mountain had shrunk to roughly half its original size. We, in the meantime, had gotten considerably closer to the object of attraction.

By the time we had reached the foot of the hill, the shadow had shrunk to a clearly defined blot about the size of a human being. It had latched itself to the undergrowth or to a tree, Just below a rocky escarpment in the center of the hill face, as if it had always been there. Still black as the night, it seemed to be leaving me with no choice, other than to pursue the line of enquiry I was following to the end.

Although I had never done the slightest bit of rock climbing or mountaineering and had no head for heights, I was determined to try and investigate the shadow. To be on the safe side, Kirsten would hold the fort at the base of the hill, while I, without further ado and gripped by the fever of the hunt, started my ascent. A couple of metres before I had reached my goal, the slope became very rugged and steep. Yet again I found myself in a situation, which, under normal circumstances and with all my wits about me, I would never have gone near.

With the last of my reserves I clambered up the rocky precipice. It was only when I was but a few metres from the edge, that I realised, what I had gotten myself into. A glance down the cliff face sufficed. All of a sudden everything else, including the shadow, was forgotten. I had reached the underneath edge of the rocky precipice, but for the life of me I hadn't the slightest idea, how I might manage to get up over the last one and a half metres. The view beneath my feet was daunting. I didn't recall the cliff face looking that steep, when I was going up it. If the way forward appeared unmanageable, the way back down was an absolute non-runner.

Instinctively and before panic took complete control of me, I turned my concentration to my immediate surroundings and began desperately searching the rock face in front of me. As my knees sagged, my hands gripped the rocky ledge fiercely. As luck would have it, I noticed a reasonably thick piece of root, which had grown over the edge of the precipice and attached itself to the soil there. Being about the size of a handle, one finds on subway trains, I made a grab for it. The notion, that it might break or rip apart, only came to me after I was hanging from its tough loop.

For a brief, dizzy moment my legs dangled free in the air. Then my feet found a toehold and I was able to support my body weight again, this time somewhat better. I took the opportunity to wave quickly with one of my arms, in order to signal to Kirsten my predicament. This exertion didn't last very long. Clinging fearfully to my root-cum-strap, I felt stuck between heaven and earth. My body, which seemingly didn't need any more information, rebelled and strained itself in every direction. Drawing upon my growing fear and anger and using my hands and legs in a monkey-like fashion, I managed to climb one body length higher. I took hold of some undergrowth and pulled myself onto a little hollow in the rockface. On this horizontal surface, along with the bit of undergrowth, a little pine tree was growing. After two or three gasps of breath a glance down into the abyss below brought me back to the brink of despair.

There I sat, safely on the side of the mountain, with no idea how to get any further up or down. My attempt to locate Kirsten visually made me feel dizzy. The same thing happened, when I looked above me. In the blink of an eye I resigned myself to remaining sitting where I was. Pressing my posterior with as much force as possible against the ledge had nothing to do with self-abandonment or resignation to my fate. On the contrary, I was hoping to be rescued extraneously. I envisioned the local rescue services being able to extricate me somehow. The consideration, that these volunteers would have to make an enormous effort in terms of time as well as of human and technical ressources, to liberate me from my predicament, was something which fortunately had not dawned upon me yet.

Gradually, my situation mutated into a kind of self-forgotten solitude, the like of which I had heretofore never experienced. Unsurprisingly, perhaps, I had begun at some stage to rock myself back and forth in an endorphin-induced state of ecstasy.

The fact, that my increasingly warm hands had acquired a firm grasp on the undergrowth, produced a feeling of security, which at that moment every part of me experienced with incomparable intensity. I was overcome by the unmistakeable feeling, that everything in this place and its surroundings was providing me with the ultimate assurance, that at this particular location I hadn't the least reason to fear or suffer anything. This sense of security, like as if I had never been left to my own devices before, was imbuing me with the freedom to do anything, which a person under normal circumstances would be incapable of even attempting. The knowledge, that, as long as I was in these surroundings in general and this shadow in particular and regardless of what I did or didn't do, absolutely nothing harmful could befall me, carried enormous weight. The experience of being completely protected, was not just a mere feeling or promise, but manifested itself as real and immediate. Before the thought had even crossed my mind, I had already started my descent. Sliding and jumping in parts I arrived at the bottom of the hill, where Kirsten was standing.

How I ever managed to climb back down over the cliff-edge and what actually happened up there are questions I no longer bother my head with. This is something, I'm sure the reader can appreciate.

On the remaining walk to the Northern Highway Kirsten told me, that, having waved to her from the side of the mountain, I had disappeared into the small shadow, and that thereafter she had seen nothing more of me, until I suddenly reappeared beside her.

The Northern Lights
(Part 3)

In the last two weeks of our Lapland adventure we had our first exposure to the much celebrated and rightly famous Northern Lights.

Although we had studied numerous books and read various descriptions of the Northern Lights in advance, the surprising thing about our first experience of this extraordinary natural phenomenon was, that we initially didn't recognise it as such. We noticed initially merely the electrically charged atmosphere. The night sky became filled by a sort of mildly radiant fog. This mist seemed to generate its own glow, which moved across the sky with unexpected speed and changed its shape with even greater rapidity, reminding us of giant smoke rings or threads. The Northern Lights, which at this stage were only at the start of their wintery rebirth, were accompanied by a most disturbing and excruciating tension in the air. The resulting unrest drove Kirsten and me, and that not for the last time either, away from the protective comfort of the fireplace in our cabin out into the open air. We were convinced, that an almost silent noise along with strange goings-on were impelling us, to check, that everything outside was in order. For a moment, we thought that perhaps the large, black bird was up to his usual mischief on the roof of the cabin. In this night we didn't get much sleep.

The following days were dominated by the Northern Lights and the impressions they made to such a degree, that we found ourselves unable to distinguish the suspenseful events closely linked with them from those ones, which in the preceding weeks had similarly preoccupied and captivated us. In that sense, the incomparable natural occurences in our last days in Lapland blended seemlessly with the earlier strange encounters, which could not simply be dismissed.

On the day we were leaving, which just happened not to be a Monday, we set off on our long walk through the wood to the bus stop on the Northern Highway, in order to travel from there to Inari. There we hoped to get our onward connection and buy a couple of things for the trip south. With an icy demeanor we moved quickly and silently along the path we had come to know, without looking either right or left.

Perhaps it had something to do with the unusually early time of our departure or the fact, that it wasn't the day of the week we normally passed through this part of the wood; at any rate on this morning there were birds to accompany us along the trail.

We purchased our tickets in Inari for the trip to Helsinki - with the bus as far as Rovaniemi and from there with the train to the capital - and checked the departure time. With about an hour to spare, we went about our final undertakings in the little township.

In the post office, in which we used to collect our weekly mail and send any letters we had written, the friendly postmistress informed us, that we were expected in the local pub, where there was a parcel for us to collect.

Although we couldn't make any sense of this, out of curiosity we set off across the large square, where the morning traffic was just getting going and the buses were lining up, in the direction of the bari. With many other pedestrians

about, we managed, without being noticed, to reach the display window, through
which we were used to observing the
square's goings on and warming ourselves up, before catching the bus back to
our cabin. Before we knew it, the landlord had already seen us and was waving
at us frantically to come in to the bari.
On the counter in front of him lay a long-
ish well-wrapped parcel and it looked as
if it was the object, which we were to collect from, of all people, the owner, innkeeper and waiter of our pub-cum-cafe.

After nodding clearly and in the affirmative to the publican, I pulled Kirsten
aside and informed her with urgency of
my decision, that under no condition
was I prepared to go into the bari at this
particular time. Without further ado we
distanced ourselves sidewards from the
display window and crossed the square
hastily in the direction we had come. We
were fortunate, that on the other side of
the square there was a little grocery
store. We dived in there, as if a visit to
this establishment had been our intention all along.

As behoves tourists, we immediately
started examining the various items on

display on the shelves, in the baskets and on the little side tables. Every now and again, I would take a glimpse through the window out at the square, which, although slowly filling up with busses, private cars and pedestrians, was still possible to overview. To suddenly make out the innkeeper with the long packet under his arm perturbed me less than the fact, that he was only progressing slowly, because he was constantly looking around, as if searching for somebody. I hadn't the slightest doubt, who he was trying to find, and so I indicated to Kirsten, that we should quickly retreat into the back of the shop. Never before had we advanced this far into the shop's dark interior. Surrounded by the tools, utility objects and household goods, which are useful for cabin and wooden house living, it was as if we'd landed in a warehouse in the Wild West. Obviously, only the front section of the little store was directed at tourists and passing trade. In the semidarkness of the shop's interior, it dawned on us, that in the course of his search the barkeeper was unlikely to overlook this store.

By the time he entered, Kirsten and I had already split up. With her hood pulled up over her head, while busily examining rubber boots of different sizes, she attempted to effect a disguise. I, on the other hand, was watching from behind a wooden shelf to see, how far the hospitable barkeeper would go. A clear, if somewhat short exchange of words took place between himself and the owner of the little supermarket. In reply to a question, which I could neither make out fully nor in the least understand, the shop owner indicated with his thumb towards the back of the premises. For a moment, I thought the game of hide and seek was about to end. The urgency, with which the shop owner began to explain something to the friendly barkeeper, caused their conversation to become louder and as a result some of the words carried over to me. Repeatedly I heard the shop owner say something like, "Idne, idne, idnequapas". The concern in his tone of voice was unmistakeable. It seemed to suffice for the innkeeper, and he left as suddenly as he had entered. He didn't even attempt to part with the elongated parcel or to leave it behind on the counter. Without bothering to savour my feelings of relief, I headed for the back of the shop, where I expected Kirsten was waiting.

I was so sure of finding Kirsten back there, that upon reaching the darkest corner, I didn't think twice, as I tapped the back of the slightly bent over figure softly and at the same time invitingly. Nobody can remotely imagine the terrifying shock I got, as the face of a very old woman suddenly turned towards me. The shock was not merely down to it not being Kirsten or because I had been doing my best to make myself inconspicuous, but also because the visage in front of me resembled a primordial rockface. This appalling revelation petrified me on the spot.

Just as my reflexes switched from fright to flight, the crone grabbed my upper arm so forcefully with her hand, that a vice immediately sprung to mind. The croaking sound I emitted in reaction must have been the reason, why she opened her mouth at me. I cannot imagine, that the sight of the salivating maw of a wild animal would have been as scary as this woman's slightly opened mouth with its single, visible front tooth. The gaze of her impenetrable black eyes remained silently fixed on her hand, with which she continued to hold my upper arm in a steely grip. As I looked into her eyes, the next wave of realisation threw me against the shelves.

In retrospect I can't recall, if I had my eyes open the whole time, or if I was momentarily concussed with my eyelids closed. The vision of the old woman's hand had clouded my senses so much, that it took a little while before I became aware, that there was nobody else between the dark shelves apart from myself. For a long time afterward I was haunted by the memory of the hornlike growth, which disfigured the nail and the tip of the woman's middle finger. An unusual hornlike boil the width of two pencils and about eight to ten centimetres in length had grown right over the nail of her middle finger. As I now know, with her vice-like grip she has never since actually let go of me.

I found Kirsten still standing near the rubber boots, regretting that we wouldn't have any use for two new pairs. Upon noticing my internal distress and without wasting any words, she simply seized the initiative.

By the time she had pretty much manhandled me out of the shop and with friendly encouragement gotten me as far as the bus, I was slowly beginning to come to my senses. However, it was only after we got on the bus and I had a firm seat underneath me, that I was able to relax completely. With a last glance back to try and see the bari in Inari and our friendly innkeeper, I glimpsed the sight of an old-style sled stool, which was being driven unusually fast by an old woman and as such had attracted not just my attention. I reckon, however, that I was the only one, who shuddered as a result.

The long, tedious hours travelling the tarmacadam highway and the train tracks brought us ever closer toward the south of Finland. I was astonished at the pleasant and heartwarming effect, which the sight of the radiant sun, which we were experiencing for the first time in weeks, had on my body and mind. I had never been a sun-worshipper, preferring instead the dark part of the year and its dismal weather. Therefore, this encounter with the sun threw me, as my physical and mental reaction to it was something I would never have expected. The sight of the sun's rays and the feeling of them on my skin triggered a whole series of sensory impressions, which kept me so distracted for the rest of our train journey, that the recent encounters with the darkness of the Arctic Circle receded to the back of my mind. For a while thereafter they didn't impinge either on my memory or my feelings.

Having checked onto the ferry, we were looking forward to the last leg of our trip home. Kirsten and I were determined to use the remaining time of our journey together to recapitulate in detail the various occurrences and experiences of the preceding weeks, in order potentially to draw some conclusions about how we might proceed together in the future. While neither of us was that keen on returning to civilisation with all the difficulties and problems, which lay ahead, the question remained to be answered, whether we wanted to maintain our proven partnership after the Lapland adventure, and if so, how we might go about it. It seems, the forces of nature were not prepared to accord us the necessary space for such a discussion, as the passage on the ferry from start to finish was plagued by a dreadful storm with strong winds, gusting up to force eleven, and correspondingly rough seas.

During the initial hours of howling winds and massive waves we sat in the cafeteria of the ferry, where we involuntarily found ourselves regaled by a seemingly never-ending series of heroic tales, which were imparted with enthusiasm to all and sundry by a Popeye-like sailor, who was obviously a member of the ship's crew. As the weather turned increasingly worse, he was intent on making clear to the small audience at his table, that he had survived much heavier storms aboard all kinds of lurching boats on the great oceans of this world. The unpredictable pitching of the ship and the endless flow of words out of the mouth of this sailor captivated my attention to the point of nausea. The fact that this little, wiry Popeye-like fellow with a skull the size of a tennis ball and a mouth the size of a football was enjoying with visible satisfaction both the show he was putting on as well as the lurching movements of the vessel, put the compellingly suggestive effect both were having on me on hold for an astonishing length of time.

Eventually, I felt so ill, that I was forced to leave the ship's cafeteria. I then proceeded to make the most disastrous mistake I could possibly have made on this passage under the pertaining circumstances. Overcome by seasickness at this stage, I convinced myself, that a quick shower would be just the thing to alleviate my discomfort. It didn't take long before the narrow confines of the shower cubicle in combination with the ship's heaving and swaying in every direction brought me unintentional and incomparable relief.

By the time we finally docked at Travemünde, I had been turned physically inside-out. As a consequence further communication and clarification between myself and Kirsten was not possible.

In Hamburg our respective partners and friends were already waiting for us.

The Three Mothers
(Part 1)

For me just as much as for Kirsten the return to Hamburg and all the trouble our friends went to to welcome us back seemed like the final arrival in exile. For the first time in my life I didn't feel quite at home in Hamburg and would without hesitation have seized the slightest opportunity to continue on my travels, had the newfound strangeness and bleakness of my home town not induced me to retreat for a couple of days into isolation.

Between reading the daily papers, watching television for hours on end and allowing the days slip by between breakfast time and bedtime, I succeeded in reacquainting myself with my old surroundings. During this period Kirsten and I abided strictly with the plan we had made, to, with the exception of the occasional phone call, initially not meet up in person.

The conversation, which we had at our first meeting after a week back in Hamburg, renewed our earlier companionship, as if nothing had changed. We weren't long coming to the conclusion, that neither of us had quite been able to readapt to the conditions here, which, before the trip to Lapland, while not appearing totally ideal, were at the very least infused with meaning and perspective. Our mutual misgivings had grown deeper and more pronounced. On the occasion of our reunion, it wasn't necessary for us to draw up a comprehensive negative evaluation of our return, in order to establish clearly in our own minds, that in the course of our sojourn in Lapland we had started on something together, which seemingly didn't want to let go of us. Resolving to think the matter over and to engage in a bit of soul-searching, we took leave of each other in the knowledge, that on our next rendezvous we would discuss how ultimately to pursue the path, upon which we had jointly started.

I spent the following couple of days hanging around in the nearby parks, lost in my thoughts and with my head full of questions. I didn't feel up to making appointments or engaging in conversation. On one of these afternoons, I sat for a long time, tired for no visible reason, under a large maple tree near the banks of the Alster. My eyes couldn't seem to drag themselves away from the tangle of branches and twigs, which was casting a shadow on the grassy verge of the lake. The confusion of darkness and light had on me a soporific effect, albeit interrupted by odd moments of total clarity. I have no idea, how long I succumbed to the interplay of semi-awake attentiveness and incomplete sleep or dozing. I can only remember, that at some time during my semi-comatose state the shadow of a large branch, which was hanging above my head, seemed to expand with unusual rapidity in width and depth, as if it was growing out of a mirror.

At this point, my natural sense of reality must have been somewhat impaired, as I refused to obey the imperceptible urge to give myself a violent jolt and escape the ongoing spectacle. It was as if I could sense on the back of my neck an evil-doer creeping up behind me, but was deliberately delaying my response, in order to surprise him with a sudden and unexpected action. That, at any rate, was the last thought I had, before I received between the shoulders a sudden blow, which was so powerful, that it tore my remaining hold on reality asunder like a thin thread.

When I came to, I found myself in a state of total constriction. On my wrists and legs I could feel the cold moistness of clay, which wasn't just weighing down on top of me, but had me sealed in on all sides and was exerting considerable pressure. The feeling of confinement, panic and fear, coupled with an unmistakeable sense of strangeness and inevitability, caused my internal organs to contract with uncompromising suddenness, the like of which I have never experienced before or since.

I felt myself choking. I could't breath. For reasons I can't explain, the episode in the dark, boggy forest of Inari in Finnish Lapland, during which, I'm convinced, a root grabbed and held on to me, shot into my mind.

Like as if a door somewhere had suddenly been flung open, I found myself, albeit still in shock from the blow to my back, exposed to a blast of fresh, oxygen-rich air. Simultaneously, all of the constrictions fell away and I was overcome by a sense of infinite space and a previously unknown freedom of movement. The ensuing silence had the quality of a flash of lightning in slow-motion. Until this moment, I had never actually realised, that when all motion ceases, pressure also can no longer exist. Every conceivable space, every imaginable distance revealed itself in an instant as the by-product of exploding objects and the grinding and gnashing of supernatural jaws. In summary, the entire world, if that designation is applicable, had opened up around me. It had neither an interior nor an exterior and I was incapable of differentiating between it and me. And yet with the knowledge, which currently guides my pen, I would characterise it as an endless cave of absolute concealment. Its shadow and its reflexionless light captured the deep impressions of the slightest curvature and the most minute detail in one and the same glance, while simultaneously affording and maintaining the most intensive and comprehensive overview of this world and its secrets I could ever have imagined. Maybe my powers of perception were unable to grasp fully what was happening, because what I was dealing with here was less a vision and more a far-reaching and pervasive encounter, which to this day defies any kind of meaningful comparison.

Looking back, it doesn't therefore surprise me, that my mental processes and sensory patterns formed a rudimentary kitchen out of those signals I was picking up from the surroundings. An enticing mixture of a stove's fiery-red flickering and the morning light of a verdant forest flooded my senses. Shadows and dark filaments alternated incessantly their locations. I couldn't establish with certainty, whether I was looking at a cauldron or a hearth. Regardless, the strange niche in this cavern of indefinite dimensions drew inexorably ever closer to me, until it reached the middle of a nonexistent line of sight. A threadlike shadow, which resembled a medium-sized stick being held vertically by an invisible hand, moved slowly and constantly around in a circle, the upper rim of which conjured up in me the idea of an enormous cauldron.

With reassuring softness and equally relentless might, a voice commanded me to remain standing and not to reveal with even the slightest movement any more of myself.

The Three Mothers
(Part 2)

I stood so still, it was as if I'd taken root. In the garden nothing else was moving either. Silence pertained.

The quietude was so complete, that I could clearly hear myself breathing and the echo thereof, which, in contrast to the surrounding peace of the grave, seemed terrifyingly loud. The concern, that someone or something might also be able to hear the sound of my breathing, was torturing me. Suddenly, I caught sight of the outline of what I thought was the old hag, I had encountered before in the grocery store in Inari. I wasn't quite sure, though. The apparition was scurrying like a blurry silhouette - or was it perhaps three? - with crazy leaps and bounds back and forth in the garden. I heard the voice again. It sounded like an echo or a distant murmur and I thought I could hear it whispering: "Never return through the gateway. Enter the garden from behind and you will be as welcome as you are at home. Never through the gateway; your mother's sisters would devour you."

As if on command, I sprinted off in a panic and practically deaf with fear past what I took to be a house, vegetable plots and what looked like bushes and fruit trees - just away and backward, ever further backward.

Something rammed me and I felt, as if I was slipping and sliding down a slope. In the midst of this fall, I toppled head over heels, banging at one stage my knees, which I had pulled in towards my stomach, and at another my neck, with which I was attempting to protect my head, against the unrelenting undergrowth and the hard trunks of the trees. How long I finally lay there, imagining myself sleeping in the warmth of my own bed, I've no idea. Eventually, tired of the growing stillness, I risked opening my eyes. An initial glance revealed a pleasant darkness, which awoke in me the clear and refreshing impression of a bright and starry summer night. The soothing, nocturnal cloak, in which I found myself enveloped, was dark, fresh, clear and cool. It certainly wasn't that of a summer night. With no reason for me to remain resting on the ground, I stood up. My limbs still stiff, I stumbled out of the shadow of the trees and bushes on to the wide and well-lit path of the Alster park, where I had been only a couple of hours before.

Just as I was coming to terms with my current condition and the artificial surroundings, something or somebody, initially I didn't know which, came, accompanied by the loud splintering and cracking of branches, hurtling out of the bushes about twenty metres away from me with the force of an fleeing animal, only stopping, when he or it reached one of the old-fashioned style park lamps. Next, the person ran toward me, his arms outstretched. At a distance of one or two metres, he started to make circles around me like a child, who's pretending to be an aeroplane. For a moment, I was perplexed and turned on my own axis, so that I wouldn't lose sight of him. As far as I could make out, he was of Indian or Indonesian origin. While continuing his circumnavigations and with an accent I couldn't identify, he started calling out the following words to me clearly: "Friend of the night, can you hear me? The runway lies on the coast, so fly with me, come fly with me." Making an even larger circle around me, he repeated his address, which this time wasn't so easy to understand, before suddenly coming to a halt. He mimicked with his tongue, nose and astonishingly powerful lungs the sounds of a plane engine, before dashing off with his arms outstretched, as suddenly as he had originally appeared.

For a few moments he could still be heard, before a strange stillness fell all around. Somewhat taken aback I stared after him, as I was, understandably, if not exactly prepared for, then at least not unused to surprises and anomalies. The nearby university hospital sprung to mind. Its large psychiatric unit was home to a number of poor souls, one or other of whom occasionally would wander off into the parks in that part of the city. I reminded myself, that it wasn't unusual to occasionally bump into strange people in a metropolis like Hamburg. In this case, however, my straight line of thought and my circuitous rationalisations would lead to me to err in my interpretation of what I had just witnessed.

The belated realisation, which only came some months later, could no longer alter the fact, that by failing to engage in a meaningful discussion with another human witness of that world, which I had just begun to enter, I had missed a significant opportunity for swift advancement. Clearly, it was much easier for me to accept the idea of a crazy Indian, than to cast aside my conventional expectations and projections. In view of the late hour on that particular evening, I was just relieved to be leaving the park. My wish for sleep and the benefits of forgetfulness was soon fulfilled.

With fresh elan and my senses restored, I found myself the following evening back on the promenade of the Alster park. Dusk was gradually making way for night. I had deliberately set off on this walk alone. Aimlessly I wandered through the park, feeling as if the day before lay weeks in the past. Fragmentary images from the previous evening impinged on my inner emotions. With each step my loss of orientation and memory seemed to grow. I was searching for the spot or the place, where I thought I had fallen asleep underneath a large maple tree. My attempts at recognition and recollection were overcome by a pleasant feeling of emptiness and my footsteps slowed to a cautious gait. I felt less and less capable of identifying what it was my memory was straining to hold on to. With a mixture of relief and tiredness, I was about to abandon my search for the evening and head home.

Before I knew it, the deep shadow of a large tree nearby had caught my eye. Surrounded by an impressive group of bushes, the tree's dense crown extended into the darkness of the starry sky, where the wind could be heard rustling the leaves. I lurched in its direction, somewhat uncertainly. Perhaps I actually was at the right place and was unable to visualise it clearly, because my recollections had sunk into oblivion. On quickly reaching the bushes, I found myself in the equivalent of a primeval Nordic wood, where foggy, drizzling rain enveloped me. Slipping into a state between waking up and dozing off, I was brutally and abruptly confronted with the most important thing I had either overlooked or been trying to forget. Overpowering and irrefutable, he stood there before me: a stocky dwarf with the presence of a giant. Although somewhat smaller than me in stature, his strength, self-assurance and directness surpassed mine unequivocally. Had this encounter occurred in total darkness, I might have imagined, I was after colliding with an elephant. That said, it was my attempt to actually come to terms with this being with its fuzzy-headed Afro before me, which lent the apparition a truly gigantic aspect. This realisation, however, altered not in the slightest the overpowering sense of menace and the strange force, which emanated from it. Covered in blankets and animal skins, the figure was difficult to identify as human. My inability to find or even make out a face multiplied the terror. This ogre, who moments before had been standing two metres in front of me, suddenly clapped me on the back with his two hands. As he propelled me like a little child before him away from a slowly dying fire in the dark part of the forest toward the interior of the island, I felt myself drained of all will. Resistance or flight could not have been further from my thoughts. After only a few steps, he grabbed me by my parka and dragged me along with him, deeper and deeper into the forest, whose impenetrability I could gauge in the stumbling of my feet and by the painful bangs to my legs and knees. I was so preoccupied by the diffi-culty of the terrain along with the pain and discomfort, that I neglected to keep track of how long my involuntary adven-ture was taking or how great was the dis-tance we were covering. When the pull-ing and the dragging finally came to an end, we were still in the forest. Slowly but surely, my eyes acclimatised them-selves to the darkness. In the residual light of the individual stars, whose reflection forced its way through the tree-tops, a surprisingly steep hill could be seen. More gently, than I might have expected, the Faceless One tugged me in the direction of this ridge.

There, my jaded senses received yet another jolt. Standing on a rocky plateau beside the little giant, who seemed simultaneously familiar and attentive, I tried futilely to apprehend with my eyes the vista before me: an almost blinding light of such intense brightness, that even with the greatest effort I cannot think of an example or a comparison, which would be appropriate.

I have no idea, how long the Faceless One and I stood staring incomprehensively with the help of this light into the dark abyss directly at our feet. My feeling is, that it could have been hours, days or even weeks. My inability to gauge or keep track of time had its origins undoubtedly in the deep black gloom, which was evolving before my eyes into the most incalculable emptiness, with which my watery eyes had ever been confronted. The incomparably intense light on the disappearing horizon contrasted more and more with the black maelstrom at the tip of my toes.

A primordial force like a huge hand on the back of my neck propelled me backward, away from the edge of the abyss. For a brief moment, I felt as insignificant as a flake of ash in the midst of a hurricane. The awareness awoke in me, that the sinister sucking power of the abyss, which, having already captivated my mind, was now taking control of that, which I insisted upon understanding as my body. The suction, the void and the lack of the slightest support, which had followed my sudden uprooting, combined to deny me any affirmation or recollection of my existence. As the raging suction of the black abyss grew, leaving me torn between falling and fleeing, so too did the echoes of my screaming soul.

The Abyss

I was overwhelmed by a spell of dizziness, followed by an attack of vomiting, which, while never-ending, actually passed in the blink of an eye. Or at least that's how it seemed. The idea, that, in the face of the next ordeal, the sudden distribution over a limitless surface, I might succeed in establishing or holding a fixed point, proved itself to be an illusion. The opposite was the case. I couldn't even envision an oasis of tranquility, and the stomach cramp, which followed the dizzy spell, ultimately devoured the last remnants of my painstakingly maintained internal facade. Spun by an external force, my flight accelerated immeasurably and any sense I might have had of the direction or the speed evaporated.

Similar to what everything around me was doing, I stretched myself in every possible direction. A wave, whose hum reached into the furthest corners of my remaining consciousness, took hold of me, thereby releasing a pressure, which was difficult for me to bear. To this day I don't know, if I was even able to breathe.

I do know, however, that in that moment of infernal experience I found myself carried away by indefinable forces, masses and objects, as if I had always been part of such raging and whirling accumulations. By now everything, which could be observed in the enormous abyss, had acquired the quality of falling masses.

In order to try to turn the madness against itself and to bring again a degree of predicability into play, nothing seemed more sensible to me, than to reach out with my arms and legs in the direction of some support, even at the risk of incurring a painful or mortal collision. Anything would have been acceptable to me in that moment, as long as it assisted in my escape from the accelerating advance of the fall and even if that involved great pain or a banal death.

During this indescribable plunge through the abyss, I was ready for and amenable to any and all changes or surprises, no matter how small, which might liberate me from the furious embrace, in which I found myself. I had long ago lost all sense of time, and in the endlessness of the fall I began to discern in ever greater detail grimacing faces as

148

well as human and animal body parts, which were descending alongside or flying past me in a sheer indecipherable confusion of speeds, collisions and directions. Eventually the ongoing disorder of lost horizons was alleviated by the gradual certitude of a modest, yet constant braking effect.

Due to my inner turmoil at the time, I can't say, how and when it was, that I finally became aware of having entered a state of suspense. All I can remember is, that I was in the air, near a granite-like cliff face, when a barely perceptible upward motion, itself the product of forces unknown to me, began to slow my fall. It seemed, as if I was moving gradually upward parallel to the granite wall, similar to floating in water. I felt, as if I was simultaneously within reach as well as at an incalculable distance from the surrounding, rugged rock face. Its impenetrable and tunnel-like exterior extended in all directions other than directly upwards and downwards, thereby defying initially all my attempts to escape or to take a different trajectory. After a while I noticed, that the rock face within the reach of my arm contained wild and bizarre fissures. Scanning its surface, I began to make out vast, deep holes, resembling inviting caves, and other openings of immeasurable depth and large enough to stick one's head in.

I tried to reach one of these cave openings by waving my arms and legs wildly, but failed miserably due to my miscalculating the spatial relations. I finally succeeded in wedging an arm in one of the football-sized holes. The failure to get solid ground beneath my feet in one of the cave entrances caused me, however, to again be overcome by extreme vertigo and panic.

Torn by the sensations of, on the one hand, being wedged against the cliff face and, on the other, of plunging fantastically toward the depths, it took me a painfully long time to realise, that with my hand I had seemingly gotten hold of something in the football sized hole, which might support me. The main part of my tortured body was being rocked gently up and down and side to side. At the same time, the firm grip my hand had on something wooden or root-like in the little opening, into which I had stuck my right arm up as far as my shoulder, was preventing the current from sucking me further into the terrifying maelstrom.

Suddenly, without the slightest warning, something grabbed hold of my wrist. "So you also reckon, that we're most likely to find a piece of wood here?", I asked Kirsten, under the assumption, that it was she on the other side of the boulder. I was just about to ask her to let go, when I heard her calling out to me from a distance of about fifteen metres, to repeat myself, as she hadn't heard me properly.

I don't recall, what I did first: shout or jump up and jerk my arm. At any rate, my feeling of panic grew exponentially, because whatever was gripping my hand wouldn't let go. Before I knew it, Kirsten was at my side. With a strong slap to the face she brought me to my senses. I no longer had the feeling of being held. In its place I held something in my hand, which turned out to be less of a stick and more a long wooden root, resembling a club. An urge, composed of inner tension and playful instinct, caused me suddenly to strike the large rock twice with this root, using all the power I could muster. Upon the first blow the front end of the root was left hanging off and with the second one it fell to the ground. Kirsten stooped and picked it up in her hands, as if it were some kind of tool. Sticking close together, we made our way back to the cabin.

In hindsight, I'm of the opinion, that we were very fortunate, despite bad weather and near darkness, to find our way back unharmed. Perhaps it was also due to the fact, that we had stopped relying on our visual sense of orientation and instead just let our feet guide us.

On the walk back I held the strange root segment up close to my face repeatedly, in order to get a sense of what it reminded me. It is for that reason, that I, upon getting within view of the cabin and being fairly sure, that there were no wolves trailing us, threw this clublike object with all my might back into the forest in the direction, from which we had come. Kirsten, in contrast, brought her piece of the root with her into the cabin. In this night we slept neither deeply, soundly nor well.

Fissures and Cracks

It must have been around this time, that I, probably in some sort of daydream-like stupor, found myself on the threshold of the threatening yet enticing room or cave with the giant, barrel-like cauldron sunk into the floor, which I had come across not long before. It was exactly the spot, where, to judge from my recent experiences, the three mothers dwelt. Later Leatherface would confirm this unequivocally and in words fraught with significance.

My initial hesitation soon, however, became a lurking anxiety, growing noticeably with every step I took further into the room. As if driven by an external force, I tried with great effort to get closer to the strange cauldron in the middle of the cave-like room. A remaining mixture of instinct and wit prompted me to desist. All of a sudden, the figure of an old woman, covered in sheets and cloths appeared seemingly from out of the wall on the other side of the cauldron and stood in the diffused green, grey light of the intangible room.

Her warm, pleasant sounding words, which, like the muffled blows of drumsticks, at once engulfed my hearing, causing me to shudder. "Your duties and chores remained uncompleted after your first visit. So get a move on, before the other two find you, as I am one of the three." "What ...?", was all I could reply, my mouth open in surprise. "The stock of darkness, boy, the stock of darkness and lightning must be stirred." The syllables rained down on me like drumbeats. "Stirred, how?", I asked, stuttering under the enormous strain, the trembling of my body revealing my total confusion. Her warnings filled the room, as she continued, unmoved: "Under no conditions would you, on the occasion of your last visit, have managed to escape, had you not understood the basic tenets of handling and made use of them." "What? Handling?", I exclaimed. The figure had, in the meantime, departed. In the foggy, smudgy dimness I was unable to find even the slightest vestige of her presence.

I forced myself, therefore, slowly again in the direction the cauldron. Although this time determined to get past the monstrous object sunken in the floor, I was not a little distressed to notice, that I was drawing closer to it more rapidly, than I had originally intended. I was about to correct myself and pull back slightly, when I found myself within arm's length of the stirring stick, which was being moved around by the swirls of a bubbling dirty stock and was scraping the interior rim of the vessel. An indefinable instinct impelled me to grab it. I could feel the handle and the pull of the flowing, somewhat viscous liquid. In the movement of the blubbering, dark gravy in the cauldron I experienced a kind of relief. It was, as if I too was being pulled around in a circle and with increasing speed being carried off to God only knows where.

Then the hand, which firmly held my own one enclosed over the handle of the stirring stick and had suddenly disturbed my circular obedience, let go, as I, due to a sudden realisation, began to move my hand in the opposite direction to the fluid's current, thereby ignoring its resistance. The phrase "stir and stoke" came to mind. Before I knew it, I was completely unable to differentiate between where my hand began and the handle ended.

Gigantic explosions set the edges of the infinite expanse alight, before densifying into strings, overcoming all distance and coldness and trapping particles, which despite their molecular size found their place in a vortex of enormous forces and near non-existent influences, having been moved from resting point to resting point in accordance with my will and with utmost exactitude.

"Without vows, stir, stoke". I could just about hear the abyss sing. Understanding this command literally seemed on the one hand too paltry, the aspiration to master it on the other too ambitious in terms of the elucidation of the magical understanding, which I was acquiring by means of unexpected exposure to this stirring, and also in terms of the strange hospitality of my new, yet ancient, mother. Seemingly out of nowhere, a white wave broke over my head and brought me up to speed.

Suddenly I was hit by a loud and heavy blow to the back. The force of it was so great, that I was knocked to the ground, landing on my face and stomach. I was overcome by a pain so great, that I instinctively drew my limbs in towards my torso, so as not to black out. It was only after I was able to distinguish the pain of the blow to my back from those in my knees and elbows, which I had incurred, when crashing to the ground, that I was seized by a sense of inner distress, the like of which I had never before known and which brought my mind back to the trail. After taking a couple of steps, I stood for a moment and looked around. There, where only moments before I had stood and being knocked to the ground, roughly thirty metres from my current, seemingly safe vantage point, a large and heavy branch was to be seen at a height of about half a metre above the trail. Jutting out of the pine trees, with the twilight in the background, it exuded a vitality and a massivity, as if it had always been there.

I was filled with an uncertainty, which only made the pain in my back and my sense of dread worse. In order to calm myself down, I shook my head vigorously and beat a retreat to the nearby cabin. Kirsten already had the tea going on the stove, and the warmth from inside and outside allowed me to slip into brief forgetfulness.

That night I had a visionary dream, which has remained etched in my mind to this day. I was able, amongst the many images, to recognise Leatherface immediately, despite his seemingly inherent ability to hide in the contours of one or other half-shadow. His powerful presence eclipsed everthing else. Initially, all I could hear was the babble of foreign-sounding voices. With curiosity, I listened to the unintelligible sounds and words, which were steadily getting louder. After a number of minutes listening attentively and trying fruitlessly to make sense of the rhythmic calls and stamping noises, I thought I was beginning to make sense of it all. My laborious attempt at understanding was eventually rewarded by a couple of words, which, although embedded in expanses of screaching and murmuring, I felt I could comprehend. In doing so, I found myself confronted by new and unsolvable riddles. All that remains of these fragments in my memory is the following approximation: "To separate yourself from your piece of wood is imprudent. It differs fundamentaly from all other sticks, clubs or root-chunks and for that reason you can no longer relinquish it. In my world I also call it the supremacy or bridge, which will forever connect you to the handle of the stirring stick in the cauldron of darkness and lightning, as long as you continue to wield it in your hand, like your mother taught you. Your mother, the Powerful One, descended from an ancient female dynasty, watches over you. You can never evade her grasp. Out of the wooden rod, which has always assisted powerful actions, the folk narrative in its primitive understanding created the universally familiar magic wand. In the folktale tradition this uninformed misconception of a walking staff in disguise or a hunting weapon led to its transformation into a magic wand, which ultimately comes to resemble a decorative dagger. Unfortunately, from this perspective the civilian world was able to misconstrue and reinvent the wooden stick, while paying tribute to its actual essence and function. In this conventional conception, however, its actual use by the human hand becomes impossible. Nonetheless, your mother's wooden rod will find you and you will be able to draw upon it. The Three Mothers remain firmly engaged in the deepest struggles. Since the dawn of time they have been foraging, fighting and asserting themselves without respite. They will share their fort, their home, with you as well as with your brothers and sisters. As your mother is one of The Three, who together act as one, she too, will devour the children of the other pair of sisters, if given the opportunity. Your siblings, conversely, are not merely devoted to you, but rather are bound to you by legacy and inheritance for better or for worse."

Leatherface raised his arm almost casually, as if to give me a wave of encouragement, while I believed I was hearing his voice, which was rapidly fading away, once again say the words, "Stir and grind, rub the bowl". His total disappearance was followed by an increase in the sound of traffic and urban background noise in general. I was back in my familiar surroundings.

For me just as much as for Kirsten the return to Hamburg and the trouble all our friends went to welcome us back seemed like the final arrival in exile. For the first time in my life I didn't feel quite at home in Hamburg and would without hesitation have seized the slightest opportunity to continue on my travels, had the newfound strangeness and the sadness of my home town not induced me to retreat for a couple of days into isolation.

Between reading the daily papers, watching television for hours on end and allowing the days slip by between breakfast time and bedtime, I succeeded in re-acquainting myself with my old surroundings. During this period Kirsten and I abided strictly with the plan we had made, with the exception of the occasional phone call, to initially not meet up in person.

The conversation, which we had at our first meeting after a week back in Hamburg, renewed our earlier companionship, as if nothing had changed. We weren't long coming to the conclusion, that neither of us had quite been able to readapt to the conditions here, which, before the trip to Lapland, while not appearing totally ideal, were at the very least infused with meaning and perspective. Our mutual misgivings had grown deeper and more pronounced. On the occasion of our reunion, it wasn't necessary for us to draw up a comprehensive negative evaluation of our return, in order to establish clearly in our own minds, that in the course of our sojourn in Lapland we had started on something together, which seemingly didn't want to let go of us. Resolving to think the matter over and to engage in a bit of soul-searching, we took leave of each other in the knowledge, that on our next rendezvous we would discuss how ultimately to pursue the path, upon which we had jointly started.

About the author

Helmut Barthel was born in 1951 in Hamburg. His writing career began when he was eight years of age. His impressive oeuvre consists of more than 1000 poems, sonnets and animal ballads, numerous aphorisms as well as two series with more than 100 short stories about important philosophers and founders of religious traditions from the ancient times up to the present day e.g. "A Carpenter in the Desert" ("Ein Zimmermann in der Wüste") and "The Fully Awakened One ..." ("Der Vollerwachte ..."). - The early short stories in "A Day like Tomorrow" ("Ein Tag wie morgen"), combine social and science fiction with fantastic elements and political satire, thereby providing a taste of the author's wide-ranging storytelling abilities. "Zauber Kalt" ("Sorcery Cold"), the first part of a novel trilogy, was published in 2015.

Helmut Barthel works as a publisher and editor-in-chief, in which function he has written a number of seminal articles in the areas of politics, philosophy and sport. His passion is the German language in particular in poetical form.

The Fully Awakened One, however, contradicted and said ...

(Der Vollerwachte aber widersprach und sagte ...)

by Helmut Barthel

Unapproachable, His Eminence goes his way, leaving behind in passing worthwhile advice and refreshing statements on perenially topical issues, fundamental questions of life and spiritual mysteries. With love and care he speaks out on every occasion against the one-sidedness of accepted truth and rejects uncompromisingly all pain and the complete spectrum of suffering.

A delightful read - not just for the members of the various creeds.

ISBN 978-3-925718-28-1

A Carpenter in the Desert

(Ein Zimmermann in der Wüste)

Once upon a time in Galilee ...
A humorous exegesis
of New Testament incidents

by Helmut Barthel

By means of a special kind of exegesis
Helmut Barthel presents the reader of
this collection of stories with a humorous, refreshingly modern and caustic interpretation of 14 episodes from the New
Testament concerning Jesus of Nazareth
and his followers shorn of the usual reli-
giosity and piety. A most enjoyable read
and simultaneously a voyage of discovery not just for the modern Christian but
also for believers in any faith.

ISBN 978-3-925718-35-9

Poetry Readings

(Lyrik Lesungen)

Poets' Corner
A Selection

by Helmut Barthel

The first poetry readings by Helmut Barthel have been reproduced by the MA
Publishing House in a five-volume book
series. The poems deal with a whole
range of topics including "the inner
world", "environmental, political and social issues", "myths and magic", "language and thought" and last but not least
"humour and satire".

Lyrik-Lesung 1 - 5:

ISBN 978-3-925718-29-8
ISBN 978-3-925718-30-4
ISBN 978-3-925718-31-1
ISBN 978-3-925718-32-8
ISBN 978-3-925718-33-5

Poets' Corner
Sweepings
Volume 1 and 2

(Dichterstube, Kehricht 1 und 2)

by Helmut Barthel

The two volumes "Poets' Corner, Sweepings, Volume 1 & 2" ("Dichterstube, Kehricht Band 1 und 2") consist of those other poems - in a variety of formats - and aphorisms, which were not previously published in the five-part series "Poetry Readings".

Kehricht und Fegen,
zum Entsorgen frei.
Doch halt! Von wegen!
Noch ist was dabei.

Es mahnt mich an Reste
und mein langer Blick
eröffnet das Beste
vom Dichtergeschick.
(H.B.)

Volume 1: ISBN 978-3-925718-26-7
Volume 2: ISBN 978-3-925718-27-4

A Day like Tomorrow
Mini-stories

(Ein Tag wie morgen)

by Helmut Barthel

In this visionary mixture of social and science fiction, fantastic elements and political satire are to be found stories for example about the reality of a meltdown in a civilian nuclear reactor, scientific progress in the distant future, with the help of which marginalised people in blissful determination can pave the way for their own destruction, and the difficulties involved in making human contact in a digitalised world. By the sparing use of bittersweet, critical dialogue the author addresses a number of burning societal issues: asylum procedures, the health service and an accident in a chemical plant.

The mini-stories give a good idea of Helmut Barthel's wide-ranging storytelling ability.

ISBN 978-3-925718-37-3

Zeitfracht Medien GmbH
Ferdinand-Jühlke-Straße 7
99095 Erfurt, Deutschland
produktsicherheit@kolibri360.de